AFTER EDIN - BOOK FIVE OF BEYOND THESE WALLS

A POST-APOCALYPTIC SURVIVAL THRILLER

MICHAEL ROBERTSON

Email: subscribers@michaelrobertson.co.uk

Edited by:

Terri King - http://terri-king.wix.com/editing
And
Pauline Nolet - http://www.paulinenolet.com

Cover Design by Dusty Crosley

After Edin - Book five of Beyond These Walls

Michael Robertson
© 2019 Michael Robertson

After Edin - Book five of Beyond These Walls is a work of fiction. The
characters, incidents, situations, and all dialogue are entirely a product of the
author's imagination, or are used fictitiously and are not in any way
representative of real people, places or things.

Any resemblance to persons living or dead is entirely coincidental.

Michael Robertson

EDEN

A Short Story
About The Zombie Apocalypse

RAT RUN

A POST-APOCALYPTIC TALE

Michael Robertson

Olga stepped closer to William, her hands on her hips, her chin jutting out. "We're not going anywhere until he's back!"

"Huh?" William said. "What are you talking about?"

The fiery girl threw an arm in the direction of the fallen Edin. Her face a deeper shade of crimson, she tutted. "*Max!* We're not going anywhere until he's back."

"That's good."

"What do you mean *that's good?*"

"I'm trying to agree with you. We need to wait for Max before we move on. So that's good, right? We're all on the same page. Or am I missing something?"

"Well"—her arms fell limp—"just in case you get any ideas to the contrary, we're—"

"—not going anywhere; I get it." Before Olga could go at him again, William turned his back on her. They were currently waiting in an abandoned building on the outskirts of the city. They'd climbed up to the first floor, Max helping them all get into place before he returned to the devastation of what had only recently been their home. Hard to know what the building had once looked like. The grey stone so common in the city made up the first floor, gnarled and twisted fingers of metal hanging from where it had broken off over the years. Small clumps of stone still clung to the bowed rods like dew bending blades of grass. They'd found a shadowy corner to keep them hidden from the diseased.

Another chill snapped through William, his skin tense with the promise of gooseflesh. Despite the bright midday sun, they were still a few months from summer.

Instead of relaxing with them, Matilda had scaled another floor of the ruins. She perched on the top as a lookout.

It had been about two hours since they'd last seen Max. "Are you worried about him?" William said. "Is that what it is?"

"No!" Olga balled her fists. "I'm just making sure you don't get any ideas about leaving him. *Again!*"

"I thought we'd worked this out?"

"We worked it out when we were running for our lives, but that doesn't mean I'm not still pissed at you for leaving him in the labs and lying to me."

With Artan still mute, Matilda high above him, and Olga clearly wanting a row, William turned to the ruined city and took in what he could see of the place. The sprawling ruins consisted of a wide variety of buildings. In their day, some of them must have been as large as four arenas put together, while others were as small as the pokiest houses in Edin. Broken bridges—collapsed in the middle—the fallen chunks now piles of rubble on what remained of the roads below. Grass pushed up through the cracks in the asphalt as nature slowly took back what had been placed on top of it all those years ago. The clumsy diseased ambled through the mess, their limbs twitching, their heads snapping, their jaws working as if they were desperate to articulate what they'd become: a denizen of hell. The embodiment of evil.

Although he'd rather have her by his side, Matilda keeping watch meant William didn't have to. With Edin behind them, they wouldn't be able to lower their guard often, so best to make the most of it now. He leaned against a rough wall and lost focus. Fatigue ran a dull buzzing ache through his muscles. At that moment, Matilda looked down, so he gave her a thumbs up. She nodded.

"There he is!" Olga stepped from the shadows and walked to the edge. Several diseased snarled.

"Get back," William said.

"You trying to hide from him?"

"How long is this going to go on, Olga? We made a mistake when we left him in the labs."

"One I won't let you make again."

"One we have no intention of making again."

"Because he's useful to you now?"

"Because he's a *friend*. Just like you're a friend. Like Artan's a friend …"

When Olga turned away from him and waved at the approaching Max, William softened his tone. "If you get back into the shadows, it will give Max fewer diseased to deal with. You know he feels a need to fight them all. Allow him a peaceful passage to us, yeah? Let him conserve his energy like we've been able to do for the past few hours."

Olga's small frame tensed, her lips pursing before she moved back into the shadows. She kept her attention on Max. "Happy?"

The sun glistened off Max's sweat-soaked skin as he picked a clumsy path through the ruins on what appeared to be leaden legs. His bloody sword in his right hand, a makeshift bag slung over his left shoulder. "Where are the rookies?" William said.

"Maybe he's got them to safety and left them somewhere to rest. It must be hard to lead so many of them through the city. How many did you say there were?"

"It feels like a lifetime ago now, but I counted eight before we left the national service area."

"That's a lot to lead through here in one go."

"Maybe you're right."

The scuffling of shoes against stone above them, Matilda came down from her lookout. She travelled down the wall like a spider, finding foot- and handholds that William wouldn't have seen in a million years. No matter how many times he watched her climb, it still took his breath away. She moved like she had supernatural powers. About six feet above them, she jumped off backwards, her legs bending as she landed soundlessly.

The urge to touch her surged through William, but he fought against it and let her go to Artan. She hugged her brother before pulling back, holding his shoulders, and peering into his eyes. "Are you okay?"

Artan nodded. He might not have spoken since they'd liberated him from his cell, but at least his blank glaze had given way to the warm glow of recognition. A mild day for March, yet the boy shivered as if they were in the middle of winter. Prisoner-of-war thin, he needed time to recover his mind and body.

Wails and roars, the castanet click of teeth. Olga had returned to the edge of the floor and had stepped on the metal bars protruding from it with one foot. She crouched down and stretched a hand out to take the bag from Max. While hugging it close to her, she turned away, shielding it from William. Max would decide what needed to be done with it, not him.

If he'd needed help getting up, William would have given it to him had Olga not blocked his path. But Max made light work of the relatively easy climb. The diseased around him paid him no mind as he dragged himself up onto the stone floor.

Pale and out of breath, Max fought to recover while taking the bag back from Olga. Heavy pants, he wiped his brow. "I'm not trying to kill every diseased now. There are too many of them." A sheet tied around a bulging sack of goods, he opened it to reveal bread, carrots, apples, and several flasks of water. Enough to fill their stomachs and sate their thirst—for now. Max winced. "I'm afraid it's all I could find."

After he'd sipped from the flask Max gave him, the water stale from where it must have been boiled days ago, William took an apple. "What about the kids on Phoenix's hut?"

Still fighting to regulate his breathing, Max shook his head. "Nothing. Nowhere. I searched the entire national service area."

Everything Matilda took from Max, she moved on to Artan until she'd been given two flasks, two apples, and now two loaves of bread. "And you didn't find anyone else?"

"Or any more food?" William added.

Olga pulled her shoulders back and stepped close to William. "Give the guy a break; he did the best he could. He's contributed more than you have."

"That wasn't a criticism."

"Sounded like one to me."

"I think you're just looking for an excuse."

"What's that supposed to mean?"

"You want to have a row. It's obvious."

Although she drew a breath to respond, Max cut her off. "William's right. The national service area fell fast. There shouldn't be a shortage of supplies anywhere. Not so soon after the collapse."

Her mouth slightly open, Olga let her response die while William pulled a tight-lipped smile at her.

"You think someone's raided the place?" Matilda said.

Max shrugged. "It's possible. Why would we be the only survivors? Especially if other people took a more sensible route and left the city rather than travel through it."

Matilda again: "And you think they might have rescued the rookies on Phoenix's dorm?"

"I'm not ruling anything out," Max said. "But I think it's an option we need to consider. Maybe we'll find some of Edin's survivors out here somewhere. Although, I'm hoping we don't. I'm done with Edin after everything that's happened."

William sat down on the hard stone floor, the others joining him, forming a circle around their limited supplies.

"While we're on the subject of how Edin treated us," Max said, "I wanted to ask you all to keep my invulnerability a secret. It's handy, and if I absolutely have to use it in front of other people to save our lives, I will, but I need you to trust me to use it when *I* think it's appropriate. I've had nearly six months of being someone else's property because of it and want to avoid that happening again. Okay?"

Max looked around the group, waiting for an acknowledgement from each of them in turn. After William and Matilda acquiesced with a dip of their heads, Olga nodded furiously in response to the question. Artan seemed oblivious, the boy attacking his loaf of bread like a wild animal feasting on a kill.

"Artan will keep it to himself," Matilda said.

William moved the remainder of their supplies to one side and pulled the crumpled map from his back pocket. The wrecked building shielded them from the worst of the wind, but it still lifted the edges of the sheet. Olga pressed her side down to help keep it flat.

A sprawling mess of ruins on the map, William pointed at them. "I think we're here." Farther down, on the opposite side of the ruins to Edin, sat what looked like a small community. A blue blob a fraction of the size of the once city they currently occupied. One of many on the map. "Because they haven't marked Edin on here, it's hard to get an idea of scale, but my guess is this is a community, and it's much smaller than Edin was."

Max raised his eyebrows. "Friendlier?"

"Who knows." William shrugged. "Hopefully. Unless anyone has any better ideas, I think we need to get to another settlement. We can't live outside of a society's protection indefinitely."

"Unless we build our own society," Olga said.

"There's five of us," William said. "As much as I'd love to spend the rest of my life so close to you, and I'm sure the feeling's mutual"—Olga pulled a face—"I think we need to aim higher. Edin was run by bad people serving their own needs. I don't believe everywhere's like that."

"And what if you're wrong?" Matilda said. "What if it's worse than Edin?"

The map showed tens of blue blobs of varying sizes between the ruined city they were currently in and what looked like a wall much farther south. "One of these places has to be friendly, don't you think? Did you get any more information from the woman you were locked in the cell with, Max? Anything that might help with our plans?"

Max shook his head. "She told me about a wall, which I'm guessing is this thing here." He traced the thick black line with the tip of his finger. It ran from one side of the land depicted on the map to the other. Coast to coast.

Matilda leaned over the sheet. "If that's a wall, it must be miles wide. It's about ten times the width of this city."

"At least," William said.

"She told me about a war," Max said. "But maybe she was just referring to the diseased; it was hard to work out exactly what she was saying. Other than that, we didn't really talk."

"For five months? Then what did you do?" Olga's cheeks reddened.

Max placed a hand on Olga's knee. "We ignored each other. She was quite hostile."

"That's good." A deeper flush of crimson, Olga coughed as if it would somehow clear her discomfort. "I mean, that must have been boring."

William would have let Olga squirm for longer, but Matilda pointed at the communities on the map. "What do these boxes mean?"

Each blue blob had a small box beside it. Some were mostly green with splashes of orange, but as the map went farther south, they turned redder until all the communities close to the wall were marked by an angry scarlet square. "It seems obvious," Olga said, "the redder the box, the more dangerous the community."

William said, "That's quite an assumption to make."

"Maybe," Olga replied, "but do you have anything better?"

A shake of his head, William said, "Either way, the community closest to this city has the greenest box. I'm sure we'll find out what it means soon enough. So we're agreed? We eat, we give Max some time to rest up, and then we move on, right? It might be a long road, but we need to find a new life out here."

Matilda and Max nodded. Artan continued to attack his roll, and Olga fixed on William, her lips pressed together while she chewed her apple. William folded the map, slipped it back into his pocket, and took a large bite from his small loaf of bread. Their lives might have undergone a drastic change, sending them into free fall, but at least they now had a plan.

CHAPTER 2

No way could William refuse to let Artan lead. Artan needed it, and more importantly, Matilda needed it. They had to do all they could to facilitate his returning to the boy he used to be. But he'd come close to saying something, and from the tightness around Matilda's eyes, she'd picked up on it. William reached over his shoulder and touched the handle of his sword strapped to his back as he followed the skinny boy through the ruins.

They'd been on the move for the past few hours, running from one elevated point of safety to the next. They caught their breath on the roofs of old churches, and the first, second, and sometimes third floors of fallen tower blocks. They'd even climbed the faded plastic seating of what must have once been a grand sporting arena. Like most of the city's history, the game played there had been lost to time. They'd had several small encounters with the diseased and come out unscathed.

For the first hour, William had led them, then Matilda. She only led for a short while, her expectation of the climbs the rest of them could make proving wildly unrealistic. Max had been slow and steady; Olga fast and efficient. So, of course, Artan had to take his turn.

At ground level again, the ruins once more proved to be a dizzying maze of dead ends, double backs, and surprises lurking in the shadows. The ground threatened to trip them with every step with the old sheets of metal, rocks, and cracks in the road.

The shriek of a diseased then called from a dark doorway on their right. It burst out a second later, blocking Artan's way. A lone aggressor, bloated from what must have been a life of decadence, the once man had bloody streaks down his face, his skin tinged green with rot. His mouth spread wide, revealing a black pit of infection. His arms windmilled as he charged. William drew his sword; the ring of steel echoed from the others following suit. But Artan moved fast. He drove a hacking slice into the side of the creature's face. The blade cut deep into the beast's left cheek. Dark blood spilled from the wound as it dragged Artan's sword to the ground when it fell. Artan pressed the sole of his boot against the side of its face and removed his weapon with a wet squelch. He raised it, ready to go again, the creature's blood dripping from it like tar.

Matilda stood at William's left, panting as if she'd just ended the creature herself. Olga and Max behind, all of them waited. After a few seconds of near silence, William sheathed his sword. "Well done, mate." He patted Artan's slim back. "You'll be back to your old self in no time."

"You sound surprised," Matilda said. She took the lead, stepping onto a large grey rock and jumping a gap of about four feet to the next one along.

Although they never agreed where their next checkpoint would be, it had been obvious every time. They found the tallest structure in their vicinity well before any of them ran out of breath. Artan caught up to his sister and reclaimed the lead.

He guided them to a destination like the others had before him. He ducked into what had once been a tower; like many of the other ruins, it had a rusting steel skeleton surrounded by brick-work. What remained of the floors had been constructed from the same grey rock so abundant in the ruined city.

The wrecked stairway leading to the first floor had a large gap from where the middle had collapsed. Not impossible by any stretch, but having to clear the four- or five-foot space and land three feet higher up made it trickier. Artan cleared it without breaking stride.

Matilda leaped across the gap with the same ease as her brother.

William jumped and just made it, landing on his toes. His heart kicked, but he had enough momentum to continue forwards, his knees slamming against the corner of a higher step. He bit his bottom lip to stifle his scream. He didn't need to give Matilda any more of a reason to doubt his jumping ability.

If any of the others struggled, they hid it well. But from the way they all stopped, they were as glad of the rest as him. Olga glistened with sweat, William wiping his own brow as he filled his lungs.

"I wish I'd saved some of that water now," Matilda said. From the way she looked at Artan, she clearly aimed it at him, another invitation for him to reply. If he heard her, it didn't show. Instead, the boy paced what remained of the building's first floor. At the other end, a set of unbroken stairs ran back down to the ground. A quick exit should they need it. Or an easy access should any diseased see them.

"How much longer do you think it will be before we're out of this city?" William said.

Olga said, "*You're* the one with the map."

Max cut in. "At a guess, I'd say we're maybe a third of the way through. I'm not sure the map can help us much. First, it doesn't have a scale on it, and secondly, it's not like we're running in a straight line. It'll take longer to charge from safe spot to safe spot, but I think it's the best option we have."

"Or a not-so-safe spot," Matilda said.

William's already tight lungs tightened. Curious at first, the mob idled into view at the bottom of the unbroken set of stairs. Canted stances, their clothes torn to shreds and flapping in the breeze. If he never saw a shrivelled diseased penis again ... At least ten of them in sight and god knew how many more behind.

Before anyone spoke, the diseased broke into their hellish chorus. A shrill shriek. A call to their brethren. As the one farthest back, William had to lead their escape.

The broken stairs they'd just climbed took them out of the building. Another set led up to the next floor. They'd also collapsed in the middle, the gap larger than the one he'd only just cleared.

"Go up!" Olga said.

It made sense, and anyone else in their party would have gone that way. But William ran down, back the way they came.

Olga followed. "What the hell are you doing? You should have gone *higher!*"

Too late now, William burst out of the old wreck of a tower and paused for the others to catch up. Artan at the rear, he took the gap in his stride.

The diseased on their heels, the first one made light work of the gap too. "Shit!" William said. He'd made the wrong choice.

William led them along what must have once been a main road. Littered with debris from the crumbling environment, he shimmied and darted along his mazy path. Beside him, Max opted to go over several rocks, Matilda and Artan following their immune friend's path.

Olga continued to snipe at William. "You made the wrong

choice. If this doesn't kill us, I swear I'm going to kill you myself."

Their current path might lead them out of the city, but they had a long way to go. "Why are we running?" William said. The ring of his sword from where he unsheathed it, he spun around and faced the onrushing horde. The others stopped, Max moving to the front. He had to be their first line of defence.

Max threw his sword in a wide arc, burying it in the skull of the first beast. *Crunch!* The beast turned limp as it fell. Olga stabbed the next one while Max took down his second. William stepped forward, Artan and Matilda at his side.

They dealt with the pack, William out of breath when he said, "We should have remained in the building and fought them there."

"*You* should have gone higher," Olga said. "You picked the worst place to run."

As if proving her right, their surroundings came to life. Lethargic at first as if the creatures had been woken from slumber, the scraping of bricks and the snapping, snarling fury of the diseased emerged from the environment.

"You've well and truly screwed us here," Olga said, turning one way and then the other as if trying to ascertain which creature would be their next attacker.

If only he'd been brave enough to make the jump to the second floor. "I thought this was the better choice."

"You were wrong."

"Can you two shut up?" Max said. "Arguing won't get us anywhere."

Matilda grabbed Artan's arm and dragged him away through a gap in the horde. A building as tall as the one they'd just been chased from, its side coated with a blanket of thick and waxy green leaves.

By the time William caught up, Matilda and Artan had

already climbed several feet. He waited for Olga, the diseased on her tail. Many of them tripped, one losing its shirt to a steel rod protruding from a grey rock.

When Olga reached him, a sneer on her puce face, she shook her head and scrambled up the vines. "You'd do well to worry more about yourself."

Max remained on the ground and cut a diseased down as William grabbed a thick vine, found somewhere for his foot, and started his climb.

William only slowed his ascent after he'd climbed about ten feet. The creatures gathered at the bottom, their zeal quelled by what appeared to be an acceptance of their limitations. But they were ready should someone fall.

It didn't matter how many times he'd been the focus of their crimson stares, William trembled, the strength leaving his limbs.

Matilda and Olga leaned out of the window they'd climbed through, grabbed William under each arm, and pulled him into the ruined building. They were on the second floor of what had once been a tower.

Olga stood over William with one hand on her hip. "The only way to get here is through the window, probably much like the second floor of the last building we were in. You might want to thank Matilda for getting us out of the tight spot *you* ran us into. Why didn't you go higher in the last building? Were it just you and me, I would have left you on your own."

Did Matilda know why he hadn't gone higher, or did he imagine the pity in her dark eyes? And he'd had the gall to worry about Artan leading them through the ruins.

As the last in through the window, Max remained closest to it. "I think you all might want to look at this."

The old window frame thick with vines, they all gathered around it, Olga shoving William aside to be closer to Max. The pair held hands. The air heavy with the rich reek of vegetation, they watched a smaller street than the one they'd been on. Much tighter and packed with debris, it took William a moment before he gasped. A tall and skinny kid. No wonder he'd earned his nickname of beanpole. "Trent?" Several more he didn't recognise, then a big man with long hair and an award-winning smile. "Samson? We should go to them," William said. "Maybe they're the ones who took the supplies from the national service area."

As William drew a breath to yell, Matilda's low growl cut him dead. "Stop!"

Every one of the gang carried something: wood, rocks, sheets of metal. They moved in small packs. It must have been their way of avoiding detection. The second pack were much less approachable. Led by Magma, among them they had Warrior, Crush, and—

"Ranger?" William said. "Of all the people to come out of Edin alive …"

"We should have seen it coming," Matilda said. "The boy's a damn cockroach; he can survive anything."

CHAPTER 3

"Where do you think they're taking all those supplies?" William said.

Olga tutted. "They're obviously building something, dumbass."

"Obviously. But what and where? If it's so obvious, maybe you can share your insights with us so we can make sure we avoid them."

Before Olga could counter him, Max said, "I'm guessing they're building somewhere in this city, which is good for us because as long as we can get out of here, we can leave them behind once and for all."

The sight of Ranger had quickened William's pulse. His stomach clamped tight and his breaths shortened. When they'd been on national service, he'd been dealing with the nasty little antagonist daily. The unrelenting nature of it had somehow made it easier to manage. But seeing the boy's smug face after some time away brought it all back. He moved closer to Matilda, who tensed at his proximity. Had she felt the same thing, or was she still pissed about him doubting Artan? "Of all the people to survive …" he said.

Olga shrugged. "I know, right?!"

"So what do you reckon, Artan? Where shall we go?" If William didn't know better, he would have assumed the boy had lost his hearing as well as his voice, his sallow eyes devoid of recognition. The kid he knew so well always had a conversation in him. Matilda raised an eyebrow. And why wouldn't she? Although he wanted Artan to talk as much as any of them, he couldn't blame her for seeing it as an attempt to get on her good side. "Look," William said, but before he could add anything else, the shriek of a nearby diseased derailed his attempt at reconciliation.

"We need to shut that thing up," William said, the diseased closing in on their position, its crimson glare fixed on them in the window. He stepped away with the rest of his friends. The shadows hid them from view, but the diseased had already seen them. It would take a while to forget.

Max nodded at the diseased closing in on them. The thing tripped over the landscape, hit the ground hard, but got straight back up again. "If we climb down the vines, Ranger will see us. Especially with that foetid alarm giving us away."

From the way Ranger and his crew moved through the city, if they'd heard the diseased, they thought nothing of it. But that could change in an instant. And it only needed one of them to get curious and their cover would be blown.

Cowardice had already forced William into making a bad decision that had put them all in danger. He wouldn't let it happen a second time. Fixed on a spot of flat ground about fifteen feet below, he drew his sword and stepped off the ledge to the gasps of his friends. The hard landing snapped through him. He'd pay for that later. His sword drawn, he stepped from the ruins and tapped the steel against a nearby wall, commanding the attention of the diseased.

The creature charged. It stumbled but remained on its feet. It slashed at the air, its fingers splayed.

His jaw clenched, William swung for the beast. Slightly too early, the tip of his sword ran through the front of its face, drawing a deep gash and dragging a spray of blood away from it. It did nothing to slow the thing's momentum.

With his second attack, William forced the tip of his sword into the beast's chest. It burst through the creature's back, ending the vile thing mid-stride while releasing the acrid stench of vinegar and rot. He kept his sword raised, ready for more.

Olga hung down from the second floor, reducing the drop by five feet before letting go. She landed with grace, glaring at William before moving aside for Max.

When Artan came down, Matilda still on the second floor, Olga moved closer to William and spoke so only he could hear. "Why did *you* jump down when Max could have?"

"Because Max didn't jump down, and someone needed to make sure that thing didn't give us away. It's not my place to tell him what to do."

"It probably wouldn't have given us away anyway," Olga said. "A diseased's scream in this city is hardly out of the ordinary."

"No, but it could have called more over. Besides, why risk it?"

William stepped away from the angry girl and nodded up at Matilda. "What's she doing?"

Although he aimed it at Artan, keeping his focus on the boy so it didn't look like an attempt to gain favour with Matilda, Max replied, "She's going to climb higher when they're out of sight to see where we should run to next. We have a few hours of daylight left. We need to use that time to get closer to the edge of the city and farther away from Ranger."

WILLIAM WAITED ON THE GROUND FLOOR WITH THE OTHERS while Matilda climbed several stories higher and peered out over the city before heading down to join them. Like the rest of them, she hung down and dropped, the dull ache at the base of William's back a reminder of his own haste in getting to the ground. She pointed in the direction they'd already been traveling before seeing Ranger and the others. "There's a cluster of taller buildings over that way. I'd say they're about two hours from here. I reckon we can reach them before nightfall, and from looking at the path Ranger and the others took, it should also move us farther away from them."

Artan burst to life, spinning around and throwing three quick attacks at diseased. He cut all of them down before their cries left their throats. The slack jaws of those around him, including Matilda, suggested the others hadn't seen them either. "My god, Artan," William said. "The last time I saw someone so adept at taking them down …"

Matilda grabbed William's hand and squeezed. He coughed to clear the wet lump in his throat. In his mind's eye, Hugh stared up at him from the corridor in the labs all over again. A moment of sadness before he got buried beneath the tide of foetid creatures. "Right, I think we should move on. I think Artan should take the lead with Max. Any objections?"

For once, Olga kept her thoughts to herself.

Max led them away from the building's ruins through a half-collapsed doorway. Artan went through next, Olga behind. When William stepped aside to let Matilda out, she snarled at him, "I forgive you for having your doubts about Artan, but don't ruin it by thinking you need to be chivalrous."

Now they had more than just the diseased to avoid, the gang moved with extra caution. From hiding place to hiding place, they took down the creatures that crossed their path in an attempt to keep the noise to a minimum.

William remained just ahead of Matilda while Olga took Artan's place at the front beside Max. "So you had four older brothers?" she said.

While stepping on a large rock, Max scanned their surroundings before he jumped back down. "Yeah. Drake, Sam, Matthew, and Greg."

"And they all survived national service?"

"Nuts, isn't it? I suppose our luck had to run out at some point. Although I'm glad to be away from that cell. I didn't ever think I'd get out of there."

William winced when Olga turned to him and said, "You nearly didn't."

Matilda's judgement had been sound. It took them close to two hours to get to the spot she'd set her sights on, the sun now a deep orange on the horizon. Broken stairs much like the ones they'd been chased from earlier that day, the gap they had to cross was similar. William led the way. He could make the jump; they didn't need to worry about that.

As William settled down near Matilda—but not so close he got in the way of her trying to reconnect with Artan—he said, "At least we didn't see Ranger and the others again. Hopefully we've lost them and we can get the hell out of this damn city tomorrow."

The second he leaned back against the wall—a cushion of vines coating the rough brickwork—William's eyes grew heavy. Despite the natural drop in temperature as day transitioned into evening, it promised to be a mild night. He hugged himself and closed his eyes, filling his lungs with a deep breath before letting it and the day's tension leave his body.

CHAPTER 4

His sleep restless from the cold bite in the air, the discomfort of the stone floor, and his inability to relax in an environment inhabited by the diseased meant it didn't take much to wake William. The croaky voice forced his eyes wide. The crescent moon shone down on them. No roof on the derelict building, it lit them up like a spotlight. Matilda and Artan were sitting close to one another, leaning in.

"Artan!" William sat up. "You're speaking! My god, how are you?" He laughed. "How do you feel?"

Before Artan replied, Olga kicked out a leg in William's direction. "It's not like I'm exhausted here or anything! You keep on, yeah?"

But screw Olga, she'd be pissed with him whatever he did.

His expression as blank as before, his cheeks sallow, his hair lank and greasy, almost as if it took on his current depressed state, Artan shrugged. "I need to pee."

"I'll go with you," Matilda said, reaching across and touching the back of William's arm. "We'll be back in a minute."

Max had also woken up, and as Matilda and Artan got to

their feet, William winced. "Um … Max, can you go with them too, please?"

Olga tutted.

Matilda said, "We'll be okay."

"It might be a bright night, but it's still night. There's still a thousand shadows down there. The diseased could be in any of them. I know you can look after yourself, Tilly, but I would suggest Max chaperone anyone in this situation."

"We're only going to the bottom of this building."

"Why can't he just do it here?" Olga said.

William could take her abuse when she aimed it at him, but not at Artan and Matilda. "You'd want to, would you?"

Although Olga opened her mouth, Matilda spoke first. "He can't pee in front of other people. It won't come out."

"*What the hell?*"

"Stop being a dick, Olga," Matilda said.

Olga might have complained, but Max had already got to his feet.

Matilda dropped down to the ground first, then Artan, followed by Max, Olga reaching out and holding his hand as he passed.

The second they were out of sight, Olga started again. "Why did you ask Max? Matilda can look after herself."

"You know why. Now give it a rest for once, yeah?"

When she stood up, William tensed. He didn't want to fight her, but he'd had enough of her bullshit.

Despite the venom she directed his way through her narrowed eyes, Olga walked to the window and peered out.

"The kid gets stage fright and you're going to watch him?"

"I'm not watching him, I'm making sure they don't get into any trou—"

It took a lot to stop Olga mid flow. William joined her at the window. "Shit!" Silhouettes closed in around Artan, Matilda, and Max. He counted eight, but it could be more. "Where did *they* come from?"

When Olga moved away from the window, William caught her arm.

A wild animal, Olga stepped up to him and bared her teeth. "What the hell are you doing? We need to go down there. I know you're a spineless weasel, but don't bottle it now. Especially as you just sent Max with them. Try to do the right thing for once in your pathetic life."

An argument wouldn't serve anyone. Instead, William pulled Olga back and pointed out the window.

"What am I looking at?"

A collection of fallen towers in the distance, similar to one they were currently in. "Look at the tallest of the three towers over there, and then look to the one to the left of it."

Because of his proximity to Olga, he felt the tight wind of tension turning through her as if she might pop. She then fell loose. "Damn. How many do you think there are?"

Another building on their right had another sentry positioned on it. "I've no idea, but look, there's one there, and one there—"

"And one there," Olga said.

As the gang closed in around his friends, every fibre of his being told William to run down to them, and although Olga would probably follow him, it wouldn't serve anyone. "We don't stand a chance if we go down there now."

A man's voice rang through the still city. "Drop your weapons. Now!"

"So … what?" Olga said. "We let them get taken?"

The clatter of steel sounded as Max, Matilda, and Artan discarded their swords.

"If they'd wanted them dead, they would have already killed them."

Three gang members moved in. They bound Matilda's, Artan's, and Max's hands behind their backs. The one behind Artan waited a few seconds longer as the boy continued to empty his bladder.

"Clearly not got stage fright now, has he?" Olga said. "I still think we should go to them. They might not kill them here, but there are a lot worse things than death. Especially for that pretty little thing of yours down there."

Bile churned in William's gut. "Are you trying to make this worse?"

"I'm just questioning the wisdom of holding back."

"If we follow them, we can work out where they're going and rescue them."

"I think it's a bad choice."

"Worse than us getting captured too?"

Olga ground her jaw.

"I didn't think so. It kills me to watch this happen, but we stand no chance trying to fight that lot. You need to trust me."

"Like you've done *anything* to earn my trust!"

"Change your tune, Olga. Hopefully they don't know about us, and they don't know about Max's invulnerability. If we're patient, those two things will work in our favour."

"So you're putting the responsibility on Max to fix this?"

William clenched his jaw to stifle his scream. "Will you stop fighting me about everything? Believe me, this is the hardest thing in the world, and if anything happens to Matilda, I won't ever forgive myself. But I genuinely don't believe we can help by going down there now. We need to follow them and come up with a better plan."

Although a man had spoken first, a small girl, who must have been younger than William, stepped forward. "Where is he?"

"Where's who?" Matilda had taken it on herself to speak for

the group. A good thing too; she had the sharpest wit of anyone William had met.

"Hugh!"

"How does she know Hugh?" Olga said.

Before William could comment, the girl added, "That little shit punched me when I was on guard at the national service gates. He was the one who left the gate open! The one responsible for this mess."

Olga gasped.

"He's dead," Matilda said. "He died in the city."

"Like pretty much everyone else! Death is better for him than what we had planned."

A large man stepped into the moonlight. He had red hair and a thick beard. "That's Rayne," William said.

The ex-protector pointed at Matilda. "I know you. You were always with that little prick Ranger hated. Where is he?"

"Dead," Matilda said.

"That's a shame. Normally we'd extend an olive branch to see if you wanted to join our community."

"I'd rather die than join you lot."

"She's not doing herself any favours down there," Olga said.

Rayne shook his head. "Be careful what you wish for, sweetheart. I think we should take you to Magma. See what he and his boy want to do with you."

The words plummeted through William's stomach.

While waving a broadsword at his three prisoners, Rayne said, "Move. Now."

Olga's voice crackled as she spoke in a throaty whisper. "So like I just said, why should I trust you? Is there anything else you've not told me? It's kind of a big deal that Hugh left the gate open, you know? When were you planning on sharing that with me?"

"You saw the state he was in at the end of our time on national service."

"So I'm supposed to forgive him for killing almost everyone I cared about?"

William sighed and lowered his gaze. "No, and I'm not sure I do either."

"And on top of that, you *still* decided Max wasn't worth saving the first time round? You and your little girlfriend—"

"*Don't* start on Matilda."

"Or what?"

William clamped his jaw shut.

"So you and your little girlfriend thought you'd leave Max? Even if I discount Hugh's judgement—as you said, the boy had clearly lost the plot by then—what am I to think of yours?"

Olga turned to walk away again and William grabbed her arm, harder this time. White light smashed through his vision and his cartilage crunched from where she punched him on the nose. Fire tore through his sinuses and his eyes streamed, the coppery taste of blood running down the back of his throat. He hadn't seen the punch coming, and the ring of steel didn't prepare him for the sword tip levelled at his face.

The shuffling of bricks and rubble beneath them announced the appearance of another group of people. Mostly men, six or seven of them, they must have been waiting nearby. They followed those who'd taken Matilda, Max, and Artan prisoner. Several more groups of similar sizes appeared from the dark ruins surrounding them.

A diseased's scream rose and died in the distance as another gang dispatched it.

The slow grind of steel as Olga sheathed her sword. "Okay, you were right. We would have been slaughtered down there. But don't think I've forgiven you for covering for Hugh, it's just that we have more pressing matters. So what do we do now, genius?"

His nose in a pinch to stop the blood flow, William said, "I won't let anything happen to them. I say we wait five minutes to give all the others time to expose themselves. Then we follow them."

Her face still locked with a bitter twist, Olga said, "If this goes wrong, I'm holding you responsible."

CHAPTER 5

William had to let go of his nose to climb down from the ruins. By the time he found solid ground again, blood coated his front, the fabric lying damp against his chest. While Olga descended to be beside him, he tore a small strip from the bottom of his shirt and then tore that strip in two. He twisted each piece of fabric into a tight wad before plugging each nostril. Despite the shadows surrounding them, the moonlight revealed Olga's smirk. "Idt's dot funny!"

Her face dropped. "Neither's finding out Hugh caused the collapse of Edin. And even worse, *you* deciding I didn't need to know that!"

Their view impaired now they were lower down, they waited for about a minute before Olga led them out of the ruined tower and in the direction of their friends. They both had their swords drawn, William's tired eyes stinging from trying to take in his dark surroundings.

A crescent moon in the cloudless sky, it gave them some light to plan their route out of there, but it did little to warn them of the smaller rocks and debris in the abandoned streets.

One of the metal rods tore across William's right shin. When he reached down to rub it, he grazed his knuckles on a nearby wall.

Were Olga not moving at such a pace, William might have slowed to tend to his pains, but she flew through the landscape with the grace and agility of a squirrel. Until she stopped dead.

Just as William caught up to her, she drove her sword into the darkness. The wet squelch of steel sank into flesh. The rancid reek of vinegar and rot. A diseased dropped to its knees, folded forward, and sprawled across the road.

His pulse raging, his lungs tight, William gripped his sword and waited, spinning one way and then the other. But no more diseased appeared. For now.

The gang and their friends remained out of sight. The second the diseased had fallen, Olga had set off again. William bit back the urge to call after her. How the hell did she move so easily? She traveled as if she had night vision, stepping up on rocks and leaping from one ruin to the next. William scraped his other shin, smashed his shoulder into a wall, and stumbled, nearly dropping his sword as he fought to maintain his balance.

They charged up a slight incline. The top of the hill, along with the large ruins running along it, blocked their line of sight. Was it naive to expect his friends to be just over the brow? What if they'd vanished?

Close to the ruined towers William had seen the first sentries in, he squinted, but it did little to penetrate the darkness. Hopefully they'd moved on with the rest of the gang.

The road clearer and better lit as they drew closer to the brow of the hill, William quickened his pace, catching up with Olga. And a good job too. The wind at their backs, he would have heard it much sooner had the breeze been coming towards them. He reached out to his short friend.

In his panic, he gripped too hard and Olga spun around with

her sword raised. Again. A finger pressed across his lips, he spoke in a whisper. "Listen!"

The snarl of diseased close by. The whites of Olga's eyes stood out on her face.

"They're just over the hill," William said.

Olga nodded.

William pointed at the tower they'd seen a sentry in. "We can hide out in there."

Olga nodded again, this time letting William take the lead.

The cries of multiple diseased over the brow of the hill, it sounded like a war between them and the people who'd caught Matilda, Artan, and Max. They were farther away than William had hoped. The warriors met the diseased's screams with war cries of their own. The sound of hacking and slashing, the frenzy of their joint enemy gradually quietened.

Despite not being able to see the battle, William's attention remained over the hill as he slipped through the crumbling doorway of the tower. A diseased then slammed into him, sending him stumbling as he reached out to hold it back. In his face, it smothered him with its rancid breath. Its mouth stretched wide in a scream as it leaned closer, his arms shaking from its pressure.

A flash of silver to his right, Olga stabbed the thing in the face. Another rich and sickening waft of rot and vinegar, the creature fell away.

His sword ready for the next one, the creature burst from the shadows. William chopped at its neck, bracing for the resistance of blade hitting flesh. But it never came. The thing had ducked. It ducked! "What the hell?"

The woman jumped up, screaming as loud as a diseased.

William leaped back, her sword missing his front by inches.

Olga filled the distance between them. The woman backed

into a corner, avoiding her attack. She screamed, "We have more prisoners here!"

Olga swung her sword a second time. Sparks strobed through the darkness, the clang of her blade hitting the wall.

The space too tight for William to rejoin the battle with his sword, he picked up half a brick from the ground. While wrapping a tight clench around the rough lump, he wound back and waited for a clear shot. Olga ducked the woman's next attack and he launched it.

He scored a direct hit, the *tonk* of brick against skull like he'd hit a tree. The woman remained on her feet, but she swayed.

Olga drove her sword into the woman's chest.

The woman gasped, fell against the wall, and slid to the ground. The moonlight showed her mouth still working, her eyes wide, her skin puce. Although she huffed a desperate wheeze, she had no chance of getting the gang's attention.

William's grip turned weak on the hilt of his sword. But Olga had already stabbed her, so he needed to do this. "She's a diseased, she's a diseased, she's a diseased." He tightened his fist before thrusting the tip of his blade into her temple. The bone yielded much like it would with a diseased, the woman silenced much like she would were she diseased. Yet the weight of his heart trebled in that moment. It didn't matter what he said to himself to get through, he'd just ended another human being, executed her at her most vulnerable. "Diseased are one thing," he said. "A fellow human, no matter how abhorrent …"

"Come on," Olga said, pulling on his sleeve as she spoke with a softness he'd not heard from her before. "We've not got time for remorse. We need to get out of here before they come looking for her."

William let her lead him away, his legs weak as he negotiated the ruins in search of a safer spot to hide.

CHAPTER 6

Guided by Olga, William's steps were wobbly from his strength having left him. They'd had to silence the woman, but it didn't change the fact he'd just murdered her. He stumbled on a rock in their path, his stomach lurching from where he nearly fell. They had to get away from there. Someone must have heard the woman scream.

They burst from the ruins into what had once been a main road. A pack of diseased on their right. Four of them, they screeched and William yelled as he cut one down.

Panting from where she'd dispatched the other three, Olga wrapped a tight grip on William's sleeve again and dragged him away for a second time.

They darted behind a wall on the brow of the hill. About six feet tall, it hid them from the battle raging in the valley below. Olga let go of him, sheathed her sword, and pulled herself up to peer over.

Several more diseased flashed past on William's left. They paid their fallen brethren no mind as they vanished from sight to join in the battle on the other side.

The moonlight shining off her sweating face, Olga turned to William and whispered, "You need to see this."

The top of the rough wall cut into William's hands, his arms too weak to support his weight. He dropped down again, scraping the old brickwork with the toe of his boot until he found a small protrusion to stand on. Matilda would have found the ledge instantly.

The ruins stretched out below them, dipping into a crater at least a thousand feet wide. The moon ran a highlight over the devastated landscape. At the very bottom, at the base of the bowl, Matilda, Artan, and Max remained bound. A circle of guards protected them for now.

As the diseased flooded into the crater from every side— some tripping and falling, some riding the momentum of the steep slope—the guards held their ground and dropped those who came too close. Another pack of seven diseased flashed past on William's left.

"I don't think they can keep this up," Olga said. "Sooner or later, the diseased will overwhelm them."

"But there's more guards than I thought," William said. Hard to tell in the chaos, but it looked like at least forty of them, if not more.

"They're still outnumbered by at least five to one."

"But they're holding their ground."

The guards were clearly experienced. They held a tight ring around their captives and forced the diseased to come to them.

His fatigue driven by his thundering adrenaline, William filled his lungs, the air alive with the calls of battle. "So on the plus side, I'd say they didn't hear the woman I just murdered."

"I'd say that's a safe bet. The question is if they don't keep this up, when do we try to help them?"

"You think we should go down there?"

"You think they'll get through this without our help?"

William's second deep inhale did nothing to settle him. "If we help them, we *will* get captured."

"But if we don't, will they all die down there?"

"Max won't. You think he'll use his power?"

"His hands are tied," Olga said. "It's not like revealing his immunity will have any positive impact."

Several of the guards fought as if they'd been born to take down the diseased. The poor light made it hard to tell, but judging by their thick frames and the ease with which they dispatched the things, they had to be protectors. But even for a gang of protectors, the odds were against them. "I think you're right," William said. "I can't stand here and watch them die in the hope the gang will get them out of it. A life without Matilda isn't worth living. We're better captured and alive than over half of us dead."

"I'll go with whatever you decide," Olga said.

"Really?"

"You sound surprised."

"You've given me nothing but a hard time since we left Edin."

"Oh, I still think you're a prick, and I've not forgiven you for not telling me what Hugh did. It's just there's more important things to deal with right now."

"Let's do this, then." Despite his words, William's leaden body ignored his will.

Before he found the motivation to jump down from the wall, Olga grabbed his arm and pointed across the crater. "Wait."

An army crested the other side of the hill. They'd come to the guards' rescue. They yelled a war cry that drowned out the diseased. Their weapons held aloft, they charged into battle.

"Someone must have gone to get help," Olga said.

"You think we should still go down and fight?"

"*No!* The only thing we'll add is a couple of extra bodies to their prisoner count. We should hide and follow them again when they set off."

"Where have they all come from?"

"I've got no idea, but I wouldn't mind betting we're going to find out soon enough." Olga jumped down from the wall. "Come on."

CHAPTER 7

Instead of desensitising to the shrill calls over time, William's pulse spiked with every diseased's scream. Each held the threat as the one that could break through to his friends. To Matilda. At least two hours had passed. It had been too dark, and their need to hide too urgent to find the perfect spot to wait. They'd opted for a large steel skeleton, the remains of the frame of what had once been a square building. They leaned against a small chunk of masonry. It had proven to be enough to hide them from sight as the night sky lightened with the start of a new day.

Dew clung to William's clothes, and his bottom had turned numb from sitting on the steel. He clamped his jaw, his entire body tense, his skin taut with gooseflesh. William hugged himself, but the cold had possessed his skeleton. Thank god they'd come out of the other side of winter. Even just a few weeks ago he wouldn't have lasted the night in his thin layer of clothes.

As another pack of diseased charged past to join the battle below, William's legs twitched with the urge to jump down. Only three of them, he could take them and have the pick of their ragged garments. But better to feel the chill than risk his life. He peered over the wall again. "I think they're finally slowing down."

Mist hung amongst the ruins, snaking through the low ground as if searching for somewhere to hide from the rising sun's burning rays. The battle continued, albeit at a sedate pace. The guards had clearly won. Close to one hundred strong, they now outnumbered the beasts at least three to one, but their attacks had grown clumsy, their steps lethargic. The fallen bodies of the vile creatures decorated the landscape. The daylight revealed the true extent of the massacre. William said, "Do you think they've lost many?"

"It doesn't look like it. Not enough to matter. They've managed to keep Max, Artan, and Matilda safe."

The three of them paler for the ordeal, but they were still alive. "It must be driving them nuts not being able to fight."

A small snarling pack crested the hill close to William and Olga again. They appeared with much less frequency now. How long would it be before one of them looked up and saw them? It had been a good spot in the dark, but the new day had made it much less covert.

The blue fabric of William's shirt had turned almost black where it had been soaked with his own blood. After he pulled his second nose plug out to examine it, he couldn't help but notice Olga's expression. "You still think it's funny?"

"You had it coming."

"You're lucky I didn't fight back. I would have—"

"Gotten yourself even more hurt. Don't pretend it would have played out any differently."

William pulled his trouser legs up. Angry grazes decorated the front of each shin, the wounds glistening in the sun. Scrapes ran around either side and his calves were red raw. Now he'd seen the extent of his injuries, it turned the low hum of pain into an angry, nerve-jangling buzz.

"Are you okay?" Olga said.

What did she think? But before William shot back, her eyes showed something they hadn't for some time: genuine concern. "Yeah." He nodded and let the tension slide from his frame. "I can't believe how you moved through the city. It was like you had night vision. You were hard to keep up with."

The day getting lighter with every passing minute, the sun stretching warmth through his cold body, William squinted as his sore eyes adjusted. The battle below them, although still active, had ground to a near halt. "I did wonder …"

"Huh?" Olga said.

"How they fought so well. I mean, the guards were seriously outnumbered for most of that battle. But look, there's Crush down there. And Warrior over there. And in the gang who arrived a few hours ago—"

"Magma."

"Yeah." William scoffed. "I'm not surprised Ranger isn't here though."

"Daddy's probably told him to stay at home so he doesn't do something stupid and get himself and everyone else killed."

William gasped.

"What?" Olga said.

"Remember we told you about the kids we left on the roof in national service?"

"Yeah, you saw one of them earlier, right?"

"Well, there's another one down there. See to the left of Matilda and the others, the short boy with black hair and skin as dark as mine?"

It took Olga a few seconds. "Oh yeah, I see him."

"When we were in the national service area, he saw us

moving on and could have alerted the diseased, but he let us pass."

"You think we have an ally there?"

"Maybe."

The final diseased's scream ended, the woman who killed it slumping when her victim fell. The girl who'd revealed Hugh as the one who caused the fall of the city walked over to Matilda.

William's stomach clenched.

Her face no more than an inch or two from Matilda's, the girl turned puce and she shook as if about to burst. "Just for fraternising with Hugh, you'll be punished. If he's dead like you say he is, someone else will pay the price for his mistakes. We're taking you straight to Ranger."

William squirmed where he sat.

"I heard he's sweet on you," the girl went on.

The gallop of William's pulse throbbed through his skull with a deep bass boom. The urge for violence flooded his system, winding his back and shoulders tight before it ran down his arms and he balled his fists. When Olga touched him, he flinched. A second later, he pulled a deep breath in through his nose and nodded, as much to himself as to her. "I'll keep my cool. I've done it all night, so I'll do it now. I'll store this for later. When I get hold of Ranger, I'm going to let it all out on him."

"You're sure you can keep a lid on it until then?"

"Yep."

"Good. We'll make him pay when we get to him. If we wait up here much longer, the diseased will see us."

"If we go into that crater, they'll see us."

"We can move around the outside. Track them from up here in the safety of the ruins. What do you think?"

"I'm not sure any of our options are good." William led the

way, dropping to the ground, sweeping bricks and rocks away with his feet so Olga had a good landing spot.

Soundless as she touched down, she said, "You want me to lead?"

"Yeah. Hopefully I'll stand a better chance of keeping up in daylight."

"I think it's more about stealth than speed now. We need to remain hidden, and as long as we keep them in sight, we'll be fine."

Right on her tail, William followed Olga through the ruins. They darted across open spaces, dodging rocks and jumping fallen walls before loitering in the shadows of ruined buildings, making slower progress but maintaining a line of sight to Magma's gang.

William moved to the edge of the crater again. His quickened heart rate shortened his breaths. The gang were mobilising slowly while still dealing with the diseased latecomers. For now, Matilda and the others might have had their hands tied, but they were still okay. His anxiety threatening to choke him out, he said, "They're alive and unharmed. They're alive and unharmed." If anything happened to Matilda ... "They're alive and unharmed."

As they continued their mazy path through the ruins, the hairs on the back of William's neck stood on end. Tuned into every sound, his eyes wide and alert, they stung from lack of sleep. It had been difficult between him and Olga, but seeing as he couldn't have Matilda or Artan, there were few other people he'd choose to have at his side right now. They'd get through this, and they'd get their friends away from Ranger and the others. They just needed to be patient.

CHAPTER 8

The ruins around the edge of the crater provided William with enough cover to walk close to the large bowl in the landscape without being seen. When the back end of the army vanished from sight, he moved nearer to the edge. Particles of brick dust and debris peppered his face, the strong wind fresh against his cheeks.

The bodies of diseased were strewn across the battlefield as if they'd been dropped from the clouds. They lay over rocks, were wedged between the ruined buildings, and a good proportion of them had missing limbs, heads, and had even been cut in half. When the wind picked up, the stench caught in William's throat. While pressing the back of his hand to his nose, he said, "I think this area of the city is about as clear as it'll get. There must be at least three hundred fallen diseased down there."

When Olga came to his side, she heaved before stepping away. "My god, it stinks."

William followed Olga, returning to the ruins away from the crater's edge. "I know we still have to keep our wits," he said, "but I wonder how far away the next diseased is? I think we're more likely to bump into one of Magma's army than we are one of those things. They've probably cleared a five-mile radius with how many they've taken down."

The wind pulled Olga's hair back, sending it streaming behind her. She squinted against the onslaught. Now they'd picked up their pace and the day had warmed, sweat coated William's body. The strong breeze offered little relief, and the cuts on his legs throbbed with an angry buzz.

"Mad Max."

William waited for a second, but when Olga offered him nothing more, he said, "Huh?"

"That's what they called him. His brothers. *Five* boys in one house. Imagine that. Five boys *and* a dad. His poor mum. Anyway, all five of them shared the same room because there weren't any three-bedroom places for them to move into."

"You'd think in construction they'd be able to build more space."

"You'd think. Apparently their room was just mattresses on the floor, and they kept all their clothes in the hallway." Olga screwed up her face. "I bet it stank! Being the youngest turned Max into a lunatic. Egged on by his older brothers, they'd pressure him into doing the craziest shit." She smiled. "Have you seen the scar on the inside of his right arm?"

"I don't look at him that closely."

"What's that supposed to mean?"

"Just that I don't look at him like you do."

"A simple no would have sufficed."

William smiled. "No."

"They dared him to dive through their neighbours' window." She laughed. "He was too young to know they were having sex."

"And I'm guessing his brothers were more than aware?"

"Yep. Not only did he tear a gash in his arm, because, well

… um … glass! But he landed in the middle of their hot moment. All four of his brothers got a hiding for that one."

As Olga's smile faded, William said, "We'll get them away from those people."

"I know. And we'll punish Magma and his twisted gang for even trying to screw with us in the first place."

"So what about you?" William said.

"What about me?"

"Well, you've told me about Max, what about you? Your family. What was it like before your sisters died?"

"We're bonding now?"

"*You* started this."

Olga hopped onto a large chunk of fallen wall. She turned a half circle, froze like a startled animal, and dropped into a crouch.

William's heart kicked when she slipped back down to the ground and drew her sword as she charged into the closest building.

William followed.

The place must have once been a house. It had debris scattered everywhere, but the walls still stood and the ceiling remained intact. They'd stepped into a large room. There were two smaller ones in front of them, a corridor between them. Olga took the small room on the left, William the one on the right. They were both at least ten feet from the open doorway. A grip on his sword, much like Olga, he peered around the wall and waited.

The scuff of movement outside. Someone kicked a brick and someone coughed. Olga pulled deeper into the shadows of her room. The darkness hid everything but the whites of her eyes and the glint of her blade.

"Hang on a minute!" A man's voice, it snapped through William, sending his back rigid. They were close.

Footsteps descended on their hiding spot.

William pulled back into the small room.

Someone burst into their building and William lifted his sword.

But they didn't come any farther in. A second later, the man groaned, his piss hitting the ground. William leaned around the corner. The man stood over six feet tall and had broad shoulders. He had a thick brown beard and lank greasy hair. His jaw hung loose like he'd drunk too much scrumpy.

The man then farted and William pulled back into hiding. In any other situation, he would have laughed. But the moment felt too personal. He was an intruder into this man's privacy.

Olga stepped from her hiding spot, her sword raised.

William shook his head. No! She'd give them away. But if he told her to stop, he'd give them away. And would it be best to end him now? To fight those outside before they found them? No. They didn't need to blow their cover. He flapped a hand in Olga's direction.

If she noticed, she ignored him.

He did it a second time.

Still nothing.

She stepped into the corridor between them and widened her stance.

The man continued pissing, still oblivious to his imminent end.

William finally got Olga's attention. He pointed back to where she'd come from and mouthed *get back!*

She frowned.

A more vigorous pointing into the small room. *Now!*

Olga shook her head.

A battle of wills would only end one way. He'd never met anyone with more fire in their belly. So instead, William pushed his hands together in prayer. The man passed wind again, his piss coming out faster before trickling off.

Olga's shoulders sagged and she retreated into her hiding place.

His breathing quick, William leaned against the rough brick wall and closed his eyes.

As the man left the building, a female voice snorted a laugh. "Took your time, didn't ya? What were you doing in there? Making love to yourself?"

"Yeah, while thinking about you."

"Dream on."

"I was. In it, you had a bag over your head and I took you from behind. Even then I could only just get it up."

"You're a dick!"

The laughter moved off with the group.

THEY'D ONLY SPENT A FEW EXTRA MINUTES IN THE SHADOWS OF the ruined building, but when he stepped outside, the change in light still dazzled William, blind spots flashing through his vision.

"Good call," Olga said. "In there, I mean. We would have had a fight we didn't need to have if you'd have let me attack that man." She smiled. "Although it would have stopped him farting."

William shook his head. "Damn pig."

The wind called a haunting melody through the ruins, filling the silence between them before Olga said, "It was good."

"What was good?"

"Life. Before my sisters died, I mean. I had two big sisters. They were only a few years older than me, and because they were twins, I worried I'd never feel as close to them as they were to one another. But they always included me in everything they did. I never told them my fears, but it was like they knew. They were always kind, always happy." A glaze covered her eyes and she looked away. "Sorry."

Were it Matilda, he would have hugged her. When William stepped closer to Olga, she snarled at him. "Touch me and I'll cut you down." While rubbing her nose with the back of her hand, she said, "Come on. Let's go."

Their surroundings hid potential attackers in every building and behind every rock. The crater on their left, they climbed another hill, the promise of yet more miles of devastation stretching ahead of them. Hopefully it would give them something more. A chance to do something other than follow the army.

A few feet from the hill, Olga said, "Look, I understand why you made the decisions you made, and I don't blame you for Hugh. That was his error and I can see how hard it must have been knowing what he'd done and keeping it to yourself. I shouldn't have been so harsh. These are trying times. The stress is getting to me."

"Thank you. And—"

"What the hell?" Olga said.

The pair stopped on the brow of the hill. The ruined city stretched away from them. A structure stood in the middle of it. It was at least half a mile from their current position. Large wooden stakes at least ten feet tall made up the perimeter. The tops were carved into spikes. Two huge gates at the front hung open as the army returned to their base. The place stretched three to four hundred feet wide. "It looks like a fortress," William said. "The protectors must have known about this base before Edin fell."

"I think they built it," Olga said.

"But that would have taken years."

"So much for them being heroes. I bet you all the while they were pretending to be going out and getting supplies, they were hanging out in this place. The ultimate clubhouse. They probably sat around all day while we worked shitty jobs in the city. And then they had the gall to come back and lord it over us."

"What do we do?" William said.

"We wait for them to close the gates." Olga clenched her jaw. "We wait until they've lowered their guard, and then we find a way in."

CHAPTER 9

"They must have had an escape plan all along," Olga said, William doing his best to match her pace as they jogged through the ruins. "When Edin fell, they could abandon it like proverbial rats. I wonder how many generations of protectors have been working on the place? So much for being Edin's heroes." She spat the next word as if to rid her mouth of the taste. "Bastards!"

Olga then darted from cover behind one collapsed building and charged towards another. Exposed for a few seconds as she crossed the main street, she then vanished into yet another shadowy wreck.

William followed her. They were still far from the fortress and exposed themselves as little as they had to. It would take keen eyes to spot them from this distance.

"I mean, what were they playing at? How did they sleep at night knowing they would abandon us in a heartbeat? We celebrated those snakes."

Again, Olga ran off, denying William the chance to respond once more. She vaulted a collapsed wall into the ruins of the next building, scrambled through what had once been a window

—the jagged square now framed with vines—and dropped into a low crouch as she duckwalked from the cover of one large rock to the next.

William sweated, the duckwalk setting his thighs alight with the muscle strain.

"It must have been why Magma chose Ranger to be the next apprentice. They obviously didn't want the secret to get out. Best to keep it in the family."

This time, Olga used the vines running up one of the buildings, scaling two floors before climbing through a collapsed window.

By the time William joined her, gassed from the climb, Olga stepped away, but he grabbed her before she escaped his reach. "Wait!" He leaned over his knees and gasped to fill his lungs. "I need you to slow down. We need a plan."

They were now only about one hundred feet from the tall and seemingly impenetrable perimeter surrounding the fortress. Guards peered over the spiked wall. Sentries looked for a reason to sound the horns around their necks. Smoke rose from somewhere inside.

"It's quite a cosy little set-up," Olga said. "You're right, we do need to think of a plan, because whatever happens, I'm getting in there. And before you say it, I'm not waiting until night-time to bust into the place."

"You think I'd want to wait that long?"

"You're too cautious sometimes."

"Some would say safe."

"*You* would say safe."

"Look, Olga, you need to slow down a little. Making decisions when you're this tightly wound—"

"*Tightly wound?*"

"See what I mean?"

Olga folded her arms and sniffed.

"It will only lead to trouble. I need to get to Matilda and Artan as much as you need to get to Max. We're in this together. We need to be sensible."

The gates were as tall as the fence on either side. Ten feet, maybe more. They didn't have the spiked tips of the rest of the perimeter; they didn't need them with the number of guards on watch. "Any approach to the front of this place and they'll see us from a mile away. There's a hill around the back, I wonder if we're better getting to higher ground. We might be able to see into the place and better assess what lies ahead."

Although Olga drew breath as if to reply, she held it in and dropped her gaze. "You're right. Sorry. I get so pissed off, and, I mean, look at what they've done. They've betrayed an entire city. But I get it. Thinking like that won't get us anywhere."

"We still don't know who built it. You're only assuming it was the protectors."

"It makes sense."

"That doesn't make it true."

William led the way this time, hanging down from a rusting metal bar next to them and dropping to the ground. The gentle pad of Olga's feet touched down beside him as he said, "Let's get around the back and see what's happening."

ABOUT FIFTEEN MINUTES LATER, THEY'D DUCKED AND DARTED from one hiding place to the next as they moved around the back of the complex. Every atom of William's being urged him to move quicker. What were they doing to Matilda in there? Had they already given her to Ranger? Even if he did get her out alive, what kind of damage had they inflicted on all of them? God knew Artan had already had his fill.

An old tower behind the fortress, it stood taller than most.

Four floors remained accessible to them. Although, Matilda would have made it all the way to the sixth. William led Olga to the second floor. High enough, a window in the back wall overlooked the complex. It's perimeter almost square, the same spiked and solid defence surrounded the place. "Well, it's a start at least," William said.

"What is?"

William rubbed his thick hair, dust and small chunks of masonry falling from it. "All the guards are watching the front gates."

"That's because it's the only way in."

About a quarter of the fortress had been given over as space to grow crops. "They've had this place for so long they've managed to set up a farm," William said. "I wonder if it's a community that's been here for a while and the protectors have only just come to it?" Slanted roofs jutted away from the other side of the wall closest to them. Huts of some sort. Hard to tell from their current position. It must have been where the residents slept. In the middle of the complex, a large fire burned. It had a boiling cauldron of water over one section, while over another they had a spit with what looked like roasting foxes. "That must be how they clean their water."

"I think your question about who this place belongs to has just been answered," Olga said.

Several large men and women approached the fire. The bald head of Crush, her dark skin shining in the sun. The red-headed Viking lookalike, Rayne, behind her. It stirred the bile in William's stomach. The bastard had recognised Matilda and sold her out in a heartbeat. Warrior, Axle, Hulk, and Fire also approached. They formed a line much like they'd done on national service. Militant. Dominant. They waited for Magma and his pathetic son. "Okay," William said. "I think you're right; the bastards have been selling us a lie for decades."

Even with the distance between them, Magma's deep voice carried through the ruined city. "This ain't Edin! You'd do well to remember that. This fortress belongs to the protectors. You do what we say, or you find somewhere else to live. Now, you're used to national service, so while we do have a wall and we do extend it because we have plans to grow, the work's voluntary."

The beginnings of a new section on William's left, the area had been cleared away and several large wooden fence posts driven into the ground, mapping out the space they intended to claim.

Trent's tall figure stood out in the crowd. The smaller boy from the national service area stood beside him.

"The work we expect of everyone is that you hunt," Magma said. "If you offer no value to us, you have no place here. You're free to leave at any time."

The crowd consisted of close to one hundred people. No sign of Matilda, Max, or Artan.

Magma walked through them and counted from one to ten, touching the head of a different person with every number. The small kid from the national service area flinched at being number ten. "We have a hunting party due back soon. When they return, you lot need to go out. We keep going while we have daylight. Whatever else happens, we refuse to run out of food or water." The cauldron continued to bubble beside him.

The screech of diseased behind them, William and Olga spun around. A pack of about ten people on the run. Men, women, boys, and girls. Several of them carried dead animals, and all of them carried spears. As many diseased as there were hunters. Although the hunters had a lead, the foetid creatures were gaining on them. "Look," William said.

Olga gasped when she followed where he pointed. "Samson!"

As one of the men in the hunting party, Samson ran at the edge of the pack, tearing through the ruins by jumping, dodging, and ducking the obstructions in his path. "Jeez," William said, "I wouldn't have expected him to move that fast."

"Maybe that's how he ended up here. There has to be something about him that got him out of Edin."

It made sense. "I've got an idea!" William jumped down to the next floor.

Olga landed beside him a second later. "What are you doing?"

"I think I know how we can get in." He jumped to the ground floor.

"Why don't I like this plan?"

"Do you trust me?"

"No."

"You're going to have to."

"What the hell?"

"Samson's going to get us into the community."

"What? But he's one of them now. Are you *insane?*"

CHAPTER 10

When they got to the ground, William rested a hand on Olga's shoulder. "I need you to fight the diseased while I talk to Samson."

"Are you out of your mind?"

"You fight the diseased and I'll persuade him to help us."

She shook her head. "Why do I get the short straw?"

"Because I'm better at talking to people than you." The ruins blocked William's line of sight, so he tracked Samson through the man's heavy footsteps as he drew closer, and shifted one building to the right. Samson might have glided through the ruins like a cat, but he hit the ground like an elephant.

Hopefully, William had judged it correctly. They didn't need to be chasing after him to get his attention.

William hopped over another wall to his right into what remained of another abandoned building. No more than a footprint of the structure it used to be. Several strips of metal lay on the floor. When he stood on the end of one, the other end lifted, flipping a handful of rubble, which landed a second later with a crash.

William widened his stance and gripped his sword, his skin tightening with gooseflesh. Samson closed down on them, but behind by just a few feet came the uncoordinated stumbling charge of the diseased.

Bursting into view, Samson's skin glistened from the exertion of his run. His scowl lifted and his eyes widened.

William pointed in the direction they'd just come from, leaping back over the wall he'd just crossed. "Follow me!"

The diseased wanted the world to know they were close. Their piercing shrieks snapped William's shoulders into his neck.

Samson followed, five diseased charging into the space they'd occupied only seconds previously.

Olga held back, ducking behind a wall while William passed her. Samson tripped, stumbling as he fell into the shadow cast by the building. William let him past and lunged at his diseased pursuers. Olga closed in behind them.

Of the five, Olga cut down three and William two, their warm blood turning the front of his shirt damp, mixing with the stains from where Olga had whacked him. It wouldn't be long before another wave found them.

"What the hell are you doing here?" Samson said, forcing his words through his heavy breaths. "It's dangerous; you should come into the fortress with me."

"No way!"

Samson stepped back and wiped his sweating brow with his thick forearm. He pulled his long hair from his face.

"We don't get on with Ranger and Magma," William said. "They've taken Matilda hostage."

"Why would they do that?"

"We have history from national service. It's a long story."

"Did you get Artan out of the political district?"

The next diseased's shriek pulled William's attention away

from the man. But it wasn't coming for them. "Yeah, and the district doesn't belong to the politicians anymore."

"That's one good thing to come out of this."

William nodded in the direction of the fortress. "As well as Matilda, they also have Artan and Max in there."

His large chest swelling and deflating with his breaths, Samson put his hands on his knees and leaned forwards. It took him a few seconds before he straightened again. "And Hugh, where is that mad bastard?"

The lump in William's throat choked off his words. He shook his head, his eyes itching with the start of tears. More footsteps closed in. He grabbed the big man's shoulder, his hand landing next to a dead squirrel he'd flung over it. He pulled Samson deeper into the old tower.

Two hunters shot past with three diseased on their tail.

When they were gone, William said, "We clearly don't have long. We need your help. We need to get inside the fortress so we can free the others."

"Are you insane?"

"Whatever it takes, we're getting our friends out of there, even if it means burning the place to the ground. Although we'd rather not do that. We don't have many allies inside those walls. Can you help us?"

"It's a lot to ask."

"I wouldn't be asking if we had any other options."

While shaking his head, Samson said, "Dammit, William. There is one way. The hunters enter the community through the back gate. It's busy around there when the hunters go out and come back in, but otherwise it's dead quiet. I can leave it open. But if I do, you have to promise me you won't let the diseased in. That you'll close it behind you. I'm risking a lot of innocent lives to make sure you two get in."

"We promise," William said.

"Okay, fine." Samson lifted his head as if to listen to the rest of the hunters. They were getting away from him. "The next lot of hunters will go out soon after we get in. Give it about ten minutes before you try the gate. And we never had this conversation, okay?"

Taking one of Samson's large hands in both of his, William shook it. "Thank you so much. Thank you."

"Right, I need to get going. Remember, this has nothing to do with me." After patting Olga on the shoulder, the strength of the man sending her stumbling to one side, he said, "Good luck."

Samson jumped a wall close to him, skirted around a large grey rock, and ran across a popping sheet of metal before vanishing through a crumbling doorway.

Olga stepped next to William and watched the space Samson had disappeared through. "So what do we do now?"

"We wait."

"And you trust him?"

"Do we have a choice?"

CHAPTER 11

Closer to the back wall of the fortress, but still a few hundred feet away, Olga and William had climbed to the first floor of another wreck. They might have been nearer, but the spiked wooden perimeter still stood as impenetrable, the sharp tops daring them to break in. No way could they climb over. If nothing else, they'd be seen by the guards near the front gate.

A loud snap of a freeing lock. William and Olga pulled back. A gate opened in the wall. Invisible until that moment, William said, "No wonder they don't guard it like they do the front. You'd have to know it was there to find it."

The next hunting party emerged, every one of them burdened with a reluctant hunch. Although, despite his initial reaction to being selected by Magma, the boy from the national service area stood straighter than most. If any of them were going to be coming back with a squirrel or rat, it'd be him.

The gate slammed shut. The hunting party ran straight at where William and Olga hid.

Like William, Olga clung to the cold steel upright running through the once building. They shared a ledge just large enough for both of them. After checking her feet as if the small platform could give way, Olga said, "Do you think we picked the wrong spot?"

Before William could reply, the first of the pack ran into the building below. Soon all ten of them had gathered on the ground floor. If even one of them looked up …

A slight girl with blonde hair threw her arms up and spoke with a whine. "How the hell are we supposed to bring back animals? Even our best hunters are lucky to get a pigeon or squirrel."

"We have to try," a boy said. "Going back empty-handed won't look good."

"If we even get back." A different girl this time. "At least when we lived in Edin, we only had to survive national service. In this place, we could die at any time."

The boy from the national service area looked up and William balked. A moment of eye contact, he returned his attention to the group. "Whatever happens, we need to give it a go. Standing around moaning about it won't help anyone. Come on."

At first, the group remained where they stood, but after a second or two's pause, some of them followed the boy. A few more seconds later, they cleared the building.

When they were out of sight, William said, "He's saved my life twice now. I feel like I owe him even more."

"But what can you do for him?"

"I'm not sure yet."

Olga crouched down before hanging backwards off the ledge. "Come on, let's get closer to the gate." She dropped to the ground floor.

≈

WILLIAM AND OLGA TOOK THEIR TIME BECAUSE SAMSON HAD said ten minutes. It allowed them to move with caution, scanning the ground for loose metal that could make a rattling alarm as they hid behind collapsed walls, large rocks, and fallen bridges.

The imposing wooden wall now just a short sprint away, Olga poked her head out and looked left and right. "Where are all the diseased?"

"Are you complaining?" William led them through another doorway, which took them closer to the hunters' hatch.

Olga caught up to him. "Not at all. I just find it a bit strange."

"Make the most of it. It won't be long before there's hundreds of the things again. The war must have wasted quite a few of the locals."

Before William could expound on his theory as to how many diseased had fallen in the epic battle, a *click* called across to them. The back door pulled in just by an inch or two. Enough to show it had been left open. "Come on," William said, checking both ways before he jogged to the wall.

As he reached out to open the door, Olga said, "Something about this isn't right. It's way too easy."

"I don't think you'll have to wait long for shit to get harder again. Also, what other options do we have that aren't risky?" Before Olga could counter, William pushed the gate open and ducked inside.

Adrenaline flooded William's system, his hands shaking as he locked the bolt behind them. A line of huts on their left. Their slanted roofs were the ones they'd seen when Magma had selected his next hunting party. "Where is everyone?"

"There's something seriously wrong," Olga said. "Wait!"

A small hut over by the fire. The door hung open, revealing a gap of about three inches. Samson peered out.

Large enough for the three of them, William and Olga darted into the shed. It smelled of freshly cut wood, stacks of logs against the back wall. The smoke from the nearby fire filled the dark space. Samson gave them some bread, an apple each, and a piece of jerky.

William's mouth watered as he chewed on the salty meat. He sighed and leaned against the wall, sipping on the water. "Thank you so much, Samson. I don't suppose you have any idea where Matilda and the others are?"

Olga watched on, her cheeks bulging from where she'd stuffed her mouth.

"No," the tall and once jovial man said. "You'll have to have a look around. I'd suggest hiding somewhere until night and looking then."

William shook his head. "That's hours away. Who knows what will happen to them in that time?"

"Fine." Samson shrugged. "But if you get caught—"

"Don't rat you out," Olga said. "You don't need to tell us that again."

After looking from Olga to William, Samson nodded and backed towards the door. He peered out through a crack before saying, "Good luck," and leaving.

Another chunk of salty meat, William then bit off a mouthful of bread and chewed them together. "Thank god we bumped into Samson. I think we should finish this food and then go look for them."

Olga attacked her meal, nodding at William's suggestion.

Were William any taller, he'd have to crouch in the tight space. As he chewed, he peered through a gap in the door at the huts along the back wall.

Olga knocked back the rest of her drink and placed the flask on the ground. She wiped her mouth with her forearm and joined William. "I reckon we should try to get onto the roof of those huts. If they're anywhere, they're in them."

"The guards by the gates will see us."

"Not if we remain at the back. The slant will hide us from their line of sight."

Before William could say anything else, a horn rang out from the other side of the fortress. "What the hell?"

Magma appeared a few seconds later, walking towards the fire while holding Jezebel. He used the top of his battle-axe to encourage movement from their three prisoners. Two boys and one girl, they had their hands tied behind their backs. "Thank god it's not Matilda, Artan, and Max."

"So much for searching this place," Olga said. "I'm guessing we're stuck here for the time being."

CHAPTER 12

A woman walked ahead of Magma. She barely touched five feet, but what she lacked in height, she clearly more than made up for in attitude. A monobrow hooded her dark glare. If you fed this woman scrap metal, she'd chew it up and spit nails. She had two thick and uneven bands tattooed around her neck as if she'd done them herself while intoxicated. If she had more than three teeth in her mouth, it would have taken for her to smile to reveal them. She lifted the horn to her lips again, her ruddy cheeks bulging as she blew.

The three kids walked behind the fierce woman and ahead of Magma. They couldn't have been any older than fifteen. That age had been the best time of William's life. The age Artan was now. Too young to worry about national service and old enough to enjoy his freedom. Anything felt possible then. All three kids walked with bowed heads, their cheeks sodden with their tears.

"What have they done to Max, Matilda, and Artan?" Olga said.

"I'm not sure. But I reckon Samson would have told us if he knew. What do you think about his suggestion to wait until it's dark?"

A tinge of roasting meat rode on the back of the smoke from the large fire. It filled the shed, mixing with the smell of freshly cut wood. They were already deep in the shadows, but when William retreated farther back, Olga followed him. She leaned into him, her face touching his as they peered through another gap in the wall.

Magma stopped in front of the fire before a gathering crowd. Trent stood among them, his dead eyes lacking the anxiety of many of those around him.

Two skinned and roasted deer on the spit over the fire, William salivated when Magma pulled a small knife from his belt, shaved a piece off, and slipped it into his mouth.

As Magma chewed, animal fat dribbling over his bottom lip, he took in the crowd. His shoulders squared, he lifted his greasy bearded chin. He got to eat from the deer whenever he damn well pleased. They'd best recognise that.

The horn sounded again and William jumped, startling Olga. He placed a hand on the base of her back, just where her body curved away to her bottom. He pulled back and cleared his throat, his cheeks warming as he whispered, "Sorry."

The angry woman blew the horn again. What looked like most of the community had gathered outside. About one hundred strong, Samson, like Trent, stood out among them. His voluminous hair and large frame gave him a unique silhouette.

"I still can't see Max, Matilda, or Artan," William said.

Olga sighed.

He reached down and grabbed her warm hand, the reassurance as much for himself as for her. "Don't worry; we'll find them."

She squeezed back.

Jezebel resting on his shoulder, the wide double-bladed axe just behind his head, Magma paced in front of the crowd. "Ladies and Gentlemen, boys and girls, I've brought you here to—" He shot a glance at the snivelling girl with her hands bound. "If you don't shut the hell up, you're going to be roasting on that fire next to those deer. And I won't do you the favour of killing you first. Although, I might skin you."

The mousy girl—so pale with grief her skin had turned almost transparent—bit her bottom lip and dropped her gaze.

After he'd drawn a deep breath, his wide chest swelling and falling, Magma snapped his head from side to side as if trying to relieve his tension. Silence fell across the crowd, many of them dropping their eyes when their leader turned their way.

Olga shook beside William. He kept a hold of her hand. If someone opened that door, they'd have no chance.

"First, I want to congratulate Samson and his hunting party for bringing back some meat. Squirrels, rabbits, and rats certainly aren't a feast, but they're something. At least they're contributing. It won't be long before they bring back even better prizes as they hone their skills." Magma swiped his thick hair back; so greasy it held in place. "We all need to bring something to the community, and hunters are now much more important than protectors. Good hunters will live like kings in this place. Like protectors did in Edin. There are no free rides here." As Magma turned on the three prisoners, his eyes darkening beneath his thick brow, William squirmed as if he could somehow wriggle free of his discomfort.

"So far," Magma said, pacing up and down in front of the prisoners, "you three have been *useless*. Less than useless. You're weak, so you're no good in the fields. You're a liability outside the walls. You're more likely to get your friends killed than you are to come back with animals from a hunt. And *you*!" He leaned close to the girl, a stick of a person in comparison to his powerful frame. "*You* do nothing but cry."

The girl continued to stare down, her light brown hair hanging in front of her face, her shoulders shaking. Even through the gap in the wood shelter, William saw her tears gather on the tip of her nose and fall to the ground.

Olga jumped this time at the sound of a deep bass drum. A slow and steady beat, another teenage boy appeared, the drum hanging around his neck. The thing had been carved from wood, the skin over the top covered in brown deer fur. He stepped in time with the beats, the hooded person behind him also moving in sync with his rhythm.

The hood didn't hide the person beneath. William sneered. "Ranger."

"He's not going to …"

"But what can we do?" William said. He angled his head to see the rest of the crowd as best he could. "Matilda, Max, and Artan aren't out there. We expose ourselves to help those kids and we'll never see them again."

Olga clamped such a tight squeeze on William's hand, he bit down against the sharp sting. He could have sworn some of the bones shifted.

The short and near toothless woman with the horn led one of the boys over to a stump of wood. The bulkier of the two, the boy had short hair and a squat frame. Although stocky, he had the girth of a baker rather than a farmer, much more used to sampling grains than ploughing them. His face twisted, turning him ugly with his grief. It took for William to stand on tiptoes and peer through a gap higher up to see the wooden block better. A slice of thick tree trunk, the top of it stained brown with old blood. Deep axe marks scarred it. Some of the cuts were so deep, the next beheading could split the block.

"No, please!" the boy said, twisting and turning in the grim woman's grip. She let him go and landed a haymaker on his chin. The crack of it connecting snapped William's shoulders to his ears. The boy folded to the ground.

Some of the crowd winced and dragged air in through their

clenched teeth. Many more watched on with the dull glaze of people who had seen this too many times before.

"We can't have freeloaders in this place," Magma said to the crowd. "Survival will be hard enough as it is. You make yourself worth something and you have a home for life."

Ranger might have looked the part, but his trembling frame undermined his callous appearance. The drum still beat while the angry woman pulled the kid up onto his knees and bent him over the log.

Counter to the drawn-out ceremony, Ranger wasted no time in swinging his axe at the boy.

Shunk!

The kid screamed a throat-tearing yell. The deep red gash in his neck belched dark blood.

William's toes curled and his stomach churned, but even over the insanity, he still heard Magma tut at his son.

Ranger screamed this time, a sound to rival that of the not yet decapitated kid. He threw another hacking cut at the boy. More momentum than before, it turned the kid's spasming body limp. His head fell to the ground with a soft *thud*. The drumbeat stopped.

William pulled away from the slit in the wall as they beheaded the next boy. It sounded like Ranger did a more efficient job the second time around.

"Please!" the girl screamed as the short woman dragged her to the block.

Again, William pulled away, but the girl's cries continued for longer than the boy before her.

Magma spoke again. "We'll show you mercy."

The squat woman had pulled the girl upright. The blood of the two dead boys covered her neck, face, and the front of her shirt. The deep crimson stood in stark contrast to her pale skin.

While twirling Jezebel, the large double-headed blade spinning, Magma snarled. "Now take her from my sight."

As Magma's fierce little helper led the girl away, the girl continued to fight and cry. What did they have planned for her? Would she become another toy for Ranger? William clenched his jaw. If he touched Matilda …

Back to the gathered crowd, Magma said, "We don't carry deadwood in this place." Close to the roasting deer, he sliced another piece of meat from its hide. This time he wiped his thick glistening lips with the back of his sleeve. "Now get back to it."

The crowd dispersed and William said, "We need to find the others before it's too late. We can't wait until tonight."

Olga shook, fixing William with a fiery intensity, spittle flying as she said, "And we need to make those fuckers out there pay!"

CHAPTER 13

"We need to go now," William said as he pulled back from the gap in the wall. "Every second counts."

Olga peered through. "It's still busy out there; but you're right, I don't think it will get any quieter than this." She took William's hand and dragged him from the wood shelter.

The second they were outside, Olga took off. William chased after her as they sprinted for the row of buildings lined up against the back wall. Their roofs were slanted, and, like Olga had said, they should hide them from the guards' line of sight. If he'd had a better suggestion, he would have offered it.

Although the crowd had left the fire, the two headless bodies still lay sprawled on the ground as a potent reminder of what happened to those who didn't contribute. Smoke rose from the roasting meat on the spit.

Olga reached the huts first. The lowest part of the long slanted roof stood about eight feet from the ground. Without slowing, she kicked off the wall and caught the roof before scrambling on top and vanishing from sight.

A second later, William joined her. Unlike Olga's soundless

leap, his foot hit the back wall with a *boom*. "You were right," William said as he lay down, "they can't see us from here."

"I know."

Like the walls of the wood shelter, the huts' roofs were made from trees cut in half. The flat sides faced down. Also, like the wood shelter, the logs didn't lie completely flush. It allowed them to see into the spaces below. The hut beneath them had mattresses and scraggly sheets spread out on the floor, but it lay empty. "I hope they're in one of these," William said.

The roof stretched over all the huts, the low end of it attached to the back wall. Olga led the way, her arms and legs spread wide. She kept low enough to remain from the guards' line of sight and shifted sideways like a crab.

When they reached the next hut, William had already broken into a sweat. The midday sun found a break in the clouds and pressed down on him. The pulse in his temples throbbed with the start of a dehydration headache. Fiery rods of pain spread beneath his shoulder blades. No matter how fit he considered himself, this movement hadn't ever been a part of his training regime. But if he stood up, they'd see him.

Each hut lay empty. Each one apparently providing nighttime shelter for ten to twenty people. No doubt many would sleep under the stars in the summer. The conditions were so cramped, maybe many of them had already moved outside.

The huts were about eight feet wide. From how far the roof stretched, they had maybe eight to ten huts in total. What would they do if they were all empty?

Sweat stung William's eyes and he blinked while Olga traversed the roofs of the hut ahead of him, pausing several times so he could keep up.

"Nothing in this one," Olga said and moved on to the next hut.

The penultimate hut had just six beds in it, each one raised from the ground on their own wooden frame. More space and more comfort. "This must be where the protectors stay," William said.

"But it's still empty."

William nodded for Olga to keep moving.

Someone sobbed inside the final hut. William shifted to be next to Olga and peered closer, inhaling the scent of freshly cut wood.

Just two beds in the space, Ranger sat on one, his cloth hood hanging from his grip, his shoulders hunched.

The ground damn near shook when Magma entered, his black hair a thick and greasy mane. He swayed with his steps, a swagger so fierce it was a wonder he didn't fall over. Jezebel in a two-handed grip as if he wanted an excuse to use her, he said, "What's up, boy?"

Ranger shook his head and continued to cry at the ground.

"Spit it out, son. We don't have time for this nonsense. What's wrong?"

Ranger jumped to his feet and squared up to his old man. Their thick chests touched. "What's wrong? What do you mean *what's wrong?* Have you seen what you're making me do?"

"Do you want me to put you in a hunting party?" Magma growled as he stepped forward, Ranger falling back onto the bed. "I'm running out of jobs for you. When we put you in carpentry, you almost cut your hand off. I know if I send you out on a hunt, you'll come back with nothing. You think I want to have to make an example of you in front of everyone? You have no skills in anything, so you get a job that allows me to justify keeping you here. We have no place for deadwood. You and I have to live by that example more than anyone."

Ranger hung his head again, his voice a febrile whine. "But I'm your *son.*"

"And had I known you'd be this useless, I would have drowned you at birth."

Ranger sneered at his old man. "You were lucky Mum even let you in her bed."

Magma backhanded his boy, the blow connecting with a thunderclap.

It threw Ranger to the ground. Hunched on all fours, tears stood in his eyes when he looked up at his dad, his lips twisting as he spoke. "What was that for?"

"You need to learn your place. I pulled favours to get you through the apprentice trials. I've carried you since your mum died." Magma held his hand above his head. "I've had it up to here with you. So give me an excuse to cut you loose, I dare ya."

Ranger slowly got up until he stood in front of his dad again. William's skin tingled and his body tensed, willing the boy to attack his old man. But he sat back on the bed.

"You're pathetic!" And with that, Magma left his boy sobbing and alone in his hut.

"Wow," Olga said, speaking in a hushed tone. "I almost feel sorry for him."

"I'm not there yet, but it makes sense why he's such a dick. But what about the others?"

Olga opened her mouth and then closed it again. She shrugged.

"They're not here, are they?"

"If they are, I can't tell you where."

"So what do we do?" William said.

"I think we should get out of here. It's not safe, and I'm out of ideas."

"But we won't get back in again if we do."

"Do we want to?"

William's cheeks puffed as he exhaled. The back wall

behind them, the top of it carved into spikes. The roofs of the huts were only two feet lower than them. "We could vault that."

Olga raised an eyebrow. "*I* could vault that."

"You worry about you and I'll worry about me, yeah?"

By way of reply, Olga jumped up, took a two-step run, and vaulted the back wall, vanishing from sight.

William followed her, gripping one of the spikes to propel himself over the others. Weightless from the fall, if only he'd heard the diseased scream before he'd leaped.

CHAPTER 14

As Olga fell to the ground—her sword still strapped to her back—four diseased surrounded her.

William landed on one of the creatures, the foetid beast cushioning his fall. When he rolled away from it, both his sword and the uneven ground dug into his back. The beast lunged for him before he got up, snapping yellowed teeth no more than a foot from his face. He held the thing back, his arms shaking beneath its weight.

Olga jumped up and drew her sword. While she fought the others, William brought his feet up, pushed the soles of his shoes into the creature's stomach, lifted it from the ground by rolling back, and kicked it over his head.

When the beast charged him again, William met it with a hacking blow to the side of its face. His sword buried into it with a crunch and the beast fell.

Olga kept the other three at bay with stabs and swipes, but none of her attacks were fatal.

The closest one had its back to William. He drove the tip of his blade into the base of its skull.

The opening she needed, Olga stabbed one in the face and

the next one in the chest. All four of them down, she took off into the ruins.

Every time William followed Olga up what seemed to be an impossibly tall structure, it took him back to being a kid, following in Matilda's wake as she defied gravity and sense with her bravery. This time they climbed a collapsed bridge made from the same grey rock and twisted steel littering the landscape.

The gradient so steep it burned his calves, William shook with fatigue. His feet slipped with every step. Nothing to hold on to, he placed his faith in his boots' grip.

A section of the bridge had fallen away, rusty rods of steel hanging from the broken path. It left a gap of only two feet to cross. Two feet wide, and two feet higher up. The rods were waiting to pierce his stomach like a hunter's arrow through the belly of a boar.

"You ready?" Olga said. But she didn't wait for a reply, leaping the gap and landing feet first on the grey rock on the other side. She sprinted just a few more feet and grabbed onto a large steel upright.

Matilda always told William his doubt came because he opened the door for it. If you don't stop to think, and if you let intuition guide you, you'll always do better. Become too aware of the risks and you'll magnify them. He nodded to the memory and jumped. His landing foot slipped as he fell forwards. His next foot slipped. Before he completely lost his footing, Olga reached down and caught him. She pulled him the rest of the way.

About twenty feet from the ground—the wind stronger because of their height—William's stomach tingled while he clung to the steel upright. It had been a tricky climb, but getting back down again would be much harder. "Remind me why I followed you up here again?"

The steel girder rang when Olga slapped it. "This hides us from them"—she pointed at the community they'd just left behind—"and we're about as high as we can get. It might show us something we haven't seen from the ground."

William's knuckles ached from where he clung on. They did have a better view than before. There was still plenty of space inside Magma's community, yet they were already extending it over to William's left. "It must have taken weeks just to clear the road for the extension down there."

"Especially with only a handful of workers. How long do you think they've been building the compound for? Five years? Ten?"

"Maybe even longer. Who knows how many generations of protectors have been using this place as their clubhouse."

"While they were pretending to help us out," Olga said, "they were prepping for Edin's downfall."

The lock on the back gate of the fortress clicked. The small door swung open, pulling into the compound. Two people emerged. Rayne led the way. A Viking of a man, he wore the scowl of a sadist. With him, he had—

"The girl from the fire," William said.

"But where are they taking her?"

The twisted and rusting girder hid William and Olga from Rayne's line of sight. William nodded at the protector and his prisoner. "You think we should follow them?"

"The second we step out from behind this metal, it'll blow our cover."

"He might lead us to the others."

"Maybe. But I'd rather be certain he will than risk it. How do we know where he's going? And why would he have that girl with him if he's going to see Max, Matilda, and Artan?"

The mousy girl still had her hands tied behind her back, stumbling several times from Rayne shoving her forward with his boot. On about the third or fourth shove, he pushed so hard she stumbled and tripped over a large piece of rock, falling to her knees with a yelp. William twisted where he stood. How could they stand by and watch?

Rayne leaned over the girl and screamed, "Get up, you pathetic cow. If you think this is bad, you wait."

Olga leaned forward, closer to William, as she whispered, "I wonder where he's taking her?"

Rayne clearly had little care for the diseased as he walked over a large sheet of metal, the clang an alarm to anyone who wanted to hear. A confident swagger, he held his war hammer as if it were an extension of his right arm.

The shrill call of diseased pinched the base of William's neck. Only three of them, and they had to get through Rayne to get to the girl. A deep laugh, the massive man wound his hammer back and took all three down, one after the other, using the weapon's weight to smash the beasts' skulls.

"It's hard not to be impressed by that," Olga said.

Rayne continued to smile.

"Sure"—William shrugged—"he's effective, but he looks awfully complacent for someone who's out in the wild. Surely he must have come across larger groups than three diseased at a time? Why doesn't he fear a horde? I don't care how good he is, a pack large enough would take him down in seconds."

"But it's quiet down there," Olga said.

"The war must have cleared them out."

"Maybe there's another reason."

"Like what?"

Olga shook her head. "Dunno. But I reckon there is." She pointed at Rayne. "What's he doing now?"

The metal sheet had been just another part of the devastated landscape until Rayne bent down and pulled one side. His prisoner continued to cry as she watched on, unable to get to her feet because of her bonds. The screech of steel against rock made William's teeth itch. Any more diseased in the area would be on them soon—if there were any more diseased in the area.

Rayne exposed a large pit. He pointed at the girl with his hammer. "You stay there. Trust me, you don't want me running after you if you decide to go walkabout."

The girl shook, her eyes bloodshot, her cheeks damp. Snot ran from her nose.

"You hear me?" Rayne said.

She nodded so quickly, William reached up and rubbed the back of his own neck as if he felt the pain of the action.

Rayne watched her for a few more seconds as if daring her to challenge him. He then backed into the hole, climbing down a ladder to the bottom. Ten feet deep, maybe more, the large protector then vanished from sight.

"A tunnel," Olga said. "Where do you think it leads?"

"I'm not sure, but I think this is our chance to help that girl."

"Are you mad? How will that help us get to the others?"

"Look at her, Olga."

"I am. She's pathetic. Even if we do try to save her, she'll probably be too scared to come and we'll both die in the process. Where will that leave Max, Artan, and Matilda?"

"Fine," William said, stretching his right leg down the bridge.

"Where are you going?"

"Don't worry. You stay there and look after yourself. *I'll* go and help her."

The screams of another girl burst from the tunnel. William froze.

Rayne reappeared with his protesting prisoner.

"You carry on making a noise," the large protector said, "and I'll feed you to the diseased. You hear me?"

The girl pushed her lips together and nodded. At least five feet six, she had more muscle than the mousy girl. Despite her bulk, Rayne lifted her above his head and threw her from the hole.

Her hands were also tied. She landed on her side with an "ooomph".

"And you wanted to go down there," Olga said.

Rayne threw his hammer ahead of him before climbing from the hole and picking it up again. He leaned over the downed girl. "Up! Now!"

Both girls got to their feet while Rayne dragged the metal sheet over the tunnel again. He pointed into the ruins. The girls took his direction, both of them with lowered heads, both of them clearly doing their best to stifle their cries.

"Before you say it," Olga said, "I'm not going to follow him."

"What if he leads us to Matilda and the others?"

Olga grabbed his shoulder with one hand. "You need to focus, William."

"What the hell are you talking about?"

"If Rayne just pulled a prisoner from that pit, or tunnel, or whatever the hell it is, there might be more of them down there."

It seemed so obvious now. "Like Matilda, Max, and Artan?"

"There we go. Got there in the end, didn't ya?"

While Rayne and the girls left, William studied the sheet of metal covering the tunnel. "It looks so obvious now it's been moved. The metal sheet's cleaner than the rest of the junk in the place. The area around it's not quite as loaded with debris. Do you think it leads far?"

"I hope not."

A momentary flashback to the tunnels in Edin. The diseased's screams as they closed down on them from god knew where. He shuddered. "Me too." While holding onto the rusting steel girder, he stepped on the downwards slope of the old bridge for a second time. The sharp decline turned the back of his knees weak: a slide of grey rock fifteen to twenty feet long with nothing but large chunks of debris at the bottom to halt their momentum. "I'm not sure we thought this one through, you know. I—"

Olga leaped past him, dropping into a crouch as she slid down the old bridge. The rush of her feet dragged over stone. William winced when she reached the gap. But she jumped it, landing on the other side as if it hadn't been there. She transitioned at the bottom from sliding to running, weaving through the debris at a flat-out sprint before she slowed.

Adrenaline surged through William, his grip weakening on the girder. Did she seriously expect him to do that? What other choice did he have?

William let go of the rusting steel, his feet sliding over the old rock as he hurtled towards the gap in the bridge. Thick metal bars protruded from the other side, daring him to screw up. He jumped, his stomach lurching as he crossed the gap, his arms windmilling.

Landing in a crouch on the other side, William fell forwards, his knees slamming against the bridge before he rolled onto his back, his shirt riding up, the rough road cutting into his skin. He hit the ground at the bottom, rolled several turns, and came to an abrupt halt when he slammed into a rock. One of the metal poles hung just inches from his right eye.

Olga blocked the sun when she stood over him. She smiled. "I'd give you a ten for effort."

Winded from his fall, William flipped her the bird.

"Come on, let's see what this tunnel's about."

The metal sheet must have been lighter than it looked because although William had never doubted Olga's strength, he hadn't expected her to slide it clear as easily. The scraping of metal against rock, she opened a gap wide enough to climb into the hole.

The top of the bridge all over again. If he didn't go in now, he wouldn't go in at all. William followed Olga down the rusted and buckled ladder built into the wall. The ground had been constructed from the same grey stone as the road above. Cracks ran through it. A scream behind him. An approaching diseased. He gasped and spun around. He faced a solid wall.

Olga grabbed his shoulder and he spun around again. "Are you okay?"

"Was there just a scream?"

"It's a dead end, William."

William hugged himself as if it would somehow keep a leash on his mind. He had to concentrate on what he knew to be real. "Max and I ran through the tunnels in Edin."

"I remember. Is this too much for you?"

It would have been nice to say no. A dead end behind, darkness stretching ahead. How far would they have to go? What would be waiting for them down there? How much time did they have to waste before they were too late for Matilda and the others? Were they already too late? "Can we track this thing above ground before we go down into it? We don't have anything to light our way down here. Maybe we can work out where we're going first?"

Olga drew a breath and opened her mouth. She paused. Her features softened. "Sure." She climbed the ladder out of there.

William followed, breathing more easily above ground. "Thank you."

"I wouldn't say that yet. This might be a worse option. What if we find out these tunnels stretch for miles?"

William's throat tightened. Before it got him with a two-handed grip, Olga jogged off through the ruins and he ran after her. At least there were no guards patrolling the back wall of the fortress.

The space where they were extending the compound had been picked clean of debris and waste. About twenty feet square, they were building within their means. Slow and steady. A trench marked the base for the extension. It had been dug about four feet deep. Sharpened trees had been planted around a third of the perimeter. "The digging must have been hard," William said, "but I bet this wall is much easier to build than the one outside Edin."

A hill stretched off away from them. "Why do you think they've built their fortress in a valley?" Olga said.

William shrugged. "Not the best defence, is it? I reckon they wanted to make sure they couldn't be seen from Edin. I suppose the enemy isn't as advanced as humans with weapons, and the last thing these snakes want is to be found out."

Although Olga opened her mouth, a tinkling bell stopped her.

"Where's that coming from?" William said.

The tinkle again, faint, but it rode the wind towards them. Although they'd cleared a space where they were constructing the wall, the hill ahead had the remains of buildings much like the rest of the ruined city. It gave them something to hide in on their way to the top. They could scale it without being seen from the compound. "It's coming from the other side of this hill," William said. "Come on." He darted for the ground floor of a ruined building.

When Olga caught up to him, she pressed her back to the wall, hiding from the fortress' line of sight.

They climbed the hill, moving from hiding place to hiding place. The bell continued to tinkle. A chorus of discontent joined in. The tinge of vinegar and rot. The curdling of an environment that only came from scores of diseased in the same place.

Just before they crested the hill—William's lungs tight from the climb—he stopped by a doorway and said, "You ready for this?"

Olga passed him on her way to the top.

William followed her and halted instantly. "What the hell?"

"I knew there was another reason why there weren't many diseased around," Olga said.

The bell tinkled again. The sound came from a cage in the distance. "Is that—?"

"Max, Matilda, and Artan," Olga said.

Their three friends were tied to a pole in the middle of the cage. They were bound standing up. Every time one of them shuffled, a bell on the front rang, calling to the diseased surrounding them.

William chewed on his bottom lip. "It makes sense why Max hasn't had a chance to use his invulnerability yet."

"Well, we don't have to go through the tunnel," Olga said, "but how the hell do we get through that lot?"

As much as William wanted to offer a different suggestion, he sighed and said, "We have to go through the tunnel."

"What?"

"Look behind them. It's a hole. It has to be linked."

"Are you sure you're okay to go through it?"

"You think how I feel about it matters?"

Olga shook her head. "No. I don't suppose it does."

CHAPTER 15

Several feet into the tunnel and William's chest had already wound as tight as a drum. The enclosed space threw his quickened breaths back at him with a mocking echo.

"You okay?"

How could Olga be so calm as she strolled through the darkness? The air thick with damp, William nodded. "D-d-do you think these tunnels might collapse?"

"What can we do about it if they do?"

A scuttling up ahead, William's gasp chased after it. "What's that?"

"A rat. Or a mouse. Either one is much better than a diseased."

The ceiling a few feet above was made from the same grey rock as the floor but with far fewer cracks—at least, the ceiling close to the entrance had fewer cracks; hard to tell now with so little light. "Imagine what it must have done to that girl having to wait down here. How long do you think they held her for?"

"And where have they taken them now?" Olga said.

Still out of breath, the memories of his run through the tunnels with Max lurked at the periphery of William's mind, ready to close in and smother him. A chill ran through him as an involuntary spasm, and his skin crawled.

"If they kept the girl down here," Olga said, "it has to be free of diseased."

Dizzy with his lack of oxygen, the dams in William's mind broke, his memories flooding in. The shrieks of diseased. The thunder of their steps. The cloying reek of smoke in the woodwork district. The girl crying as she burned, her small face blistering before she disappeared behind a wall of bright orange flames.

Metal screeched over rock and William halted. What little breath he had left him. The light behind them vanished, cut off from where the steel sheet got dragged back across it. "Shit!"

"Shh," Olga said. "Maybe they don't know we're down here."

"Of *course* they know we're down here."

"That's your panic talking. Surely they would have followed us? They might have thought Rayne left it open."

"Or they might have simply decided to trap us like they did the girl from earlier?"

"So what do we do?" Olga said.

"What else can we do? What we know for sure is that there's someone back that way. Whether they've seen us or not, they're there. The only thing we can do is get to the others and hope we find a way out of this."

They quickened their pace, William's feet tilting and rolling with the cracks in the ground. "At least we'll hear them if they follow u—" He bit back his yell as he stubbed his toe and stumbled forward, his knees slamming down against the hard ground.

"You okay?" Olga said.

For a few seconds, William breathed through his nose, nodding in the darkness. His scream successfully stifled, he finally said, "Yeah." He pushed off from the ground and stood up again. "Be careful of the hill."

"At least we know where we are. We must be past halfway now."

Thankfully the slope didn't have the gradient of the hill above. William's eyes stung from where he strained to see in the dark.

The screech of a diseased bounced off the walls of the tunnel. William stopped dead. Something touched his shoulder. He spun to face it.

"It's me," Olga said. "We're getting close. That was the sound of the diseased *outside* the cage. There's nothing in here."

"How can you be so sure?"

"If there were any down here, they would have come closer by now."

The ground levelled out. Light up ahead. "You're right! That must be the hole in the cage's floor."

"Wait!"

William jumped, turning to Olga. The daylight ahead helped, but it still took him a few seconds, blinking against his burning eyes to make out where she pointed. "It's another tunnel."

"It means we don't have to go back the way we came," Olga said. "If there is someone waiting for us, we can avoid them."

"But where does it lead?"

"Who knows?" Olga set off again towards the light and their friends.

The path grew lighter the closer they got to the hole. They ended up below and behind Matilda, Max, and Artan. William said, "Hey, don't look down."

Of course, all three of them turned and looked down. The

bell tinkled louder than before, the diseased screaming in response.

"I said *don't* look down. We've come to bust you out, but we need to be sly about this. Who knows if we're being watched. Can you see anyone looking on?"

The bell tinkled again as all three of them looked around.

Matilda shook her head. "It seems clear."

"Okay." Olga this time. "We need to be quick. We're going to come up and untie you. Then we need to get the hell out of here. You ready?"

Max nodded.

While holding up her right hand close to William's face, Olga mouthed her fingers' actions. *Three, two, one.*

On one, Olga climbed up first and William followed. Their friends were tied to a thick tree trunk. Vines had been plaited to make ropes. They were tied so tightly all three of their hands had turned purple.

The vines then fell loose. Olga stepped away while sheathing her sword. She jumped back down into the tunnel.

The diseased whipped into a frenzy, Max followed Olga, Artan next, and then Matilda. The dark mouth of the tunnel taunted William and he hesitated.

When William landed in the tunnel, he hugged Matilda. "I'm so glad you're okay."

They parted, William hugging Max next. When he held on to Artan, the boy stiffened.

"We've got to move fast," Max said. "They might not have been watching us, but they could have been listening and the bell has now stopped."

Olga led the way, jogging until it became too dark again. She slowed to a walk, her steps heavy. She must have done it to make her easier to follow. She took the new tunnel back.

Matilda walked beside William and after a minute or two said, "How are you? Where have you been?"

"We've been looking for you. We went into Magma's community."

"What was it like?"

"Horrible," Olga said. "Although, it helped me understand why Ranger's such a dick. With an old man like that, he has no hope."

William added, "We saw them behead two boys and take two girls away. We feared the worst for you."

"Thank you for saving us," Max said.

"You'd have—" Before Olga finished, she slammed into a wall with an "oomph".

William reached up. Cold steel above him. Rough with rust, he lifted the sheet and walked his fingers along to the edge before hooking them over and sliding it free. The light dazzled him, but his breaths came more easily with the fresh air. They'd found a way out. Thank God.

Olga pointed up. "Give me a boost. I'll see what's going on."

William joined his hands by linking his fingers, leaning down so she could step up. The grit on the soles of Olga's boot stung his palms.

After just a second, Olga pulled back down, her skin pale. "We're in Magma's community."

"Shit."

"What do you want to do?"

William shook his head. "We can't go back in there again."

"So what, then?" Max said.

"I think we take our chances back the way we came in," Olga said.

The thought of it clamped William's chest tight. "Back through the tunnels?"

"That's what I reckon. But I'll do whatever you think's best. You decide."

The others stared at William. Matilda, Max, and Artan weren't in a position to help him choose. And Olga had left it open. She would follow him through Magma's community if that was what he needed. But it would be more about his needs than the group's.

"What we know is there's tens of people up there," William said. "If we go back the way we came and there is anyone waiting for us"—he pointed up—"I don't imagine there will be as many people as there are up there." It took him a second to find the words. He reached up and slid the steel sheet into place. "Let's go back."

CHAPTER 16

William's toe dropped into a crack in the ground, sending him stumbling forwards several steps. Again. The heavy stamp of his feet called up the tunnel, rats running away from the noise.

He flinched when someone touched his back. Matilda said, "Are you okay?"

"I'm fine, thanks. Just a jagged bit of floor."

A few feet later the dull glow of daylight on their right marked the cage their friends had been held in. He led them left, deeper into the gloom and back the way he and Olga had come from.

The darkness closed in around them again as they descended the hill. William jumped for a second time in as many minutes when something touched him. When Matilda found his hand, he squeezed back. "I'm so pleased you're okay," he said. "And … uh, nothing else happened to you, did it?"

"Other than being bound and tied to a pole?"

"Yeah."

"No, that's all."

"Good. And, Artan, you're okay?"

A grunt, nothing more. "Humph."

"Max?"

When Max didn't reply, Olga tried. "Max, honey?"

"Huh?" Max said.

Olga said, "Are you okay?"

"Oh … uh … yeah, yeah, I'm fine. Why?"

William again. "You've been through a lot in the past few days."

After letting go of a hard sigh, Max said, "We all have."

William shrugged. "Doesn't make it any less real."

"Fair enough. I was just thinking about Drake."

"Your brother?" Olga said.

Max sighed again. "Yeah. I was wondering what happened to the others. What happened to my parents. You know, did it happen quickly? Which one went last and had to see it all unfold?"

"*You* did, Max."

Olga's words cut through the group, the near silence punctuated by Max's stuttered breaths, his voice cracking when he said, "Sorry."

"Don't be," Matilda said. "You need to let it out."

Despite all of them stumbling once or twice, they reached the end of the tunnel without incident. William patted the rough stone wall, cold to touch. He found the ladder rungs by whacking the back of his left hand against one. "Shit."

"You okay?" Olga said.

"Yeah." He rubbed it quickly to ease the sting. "I've found the ladder."

Olga again. "Let me go up first."

"No, we're here because *I* said we should come back, so I should go up and face whatever's there."

A wet sniff from where he clearly still struggled to control himself, Max said, "I should go up there."

"I don't think it's the diseased we need to worry about, mate. My hope is, the people who closed this back over assumed Rayne left it that way, and they were tidying up after him. Hopefully, they're long gone."

Rough and uneven with rust, the ladder rungs were colder than the wall. William grabbed one in front of him with his left hand and one higher up with his right. He missed when he tried to find a rung with his foot. He caught it on his second attempt.

When William reached up and felt the underside of the metal sheet, he pushed, grunting from the effort. "It won't budge."

"Try again," Matilda said.

The sheet held fast. "Still not budging." William climbed higher, dipped his head, and pressed the back of his shoulders to the metal sheet. He held onto the ladder rung with both hands and used the strength in his legs to push, lifting the sheet with his back, dizzy with both the angle and the effort. Daylight flooded in, his eyes stinging from the sudden adjustment. "Got it!"

Olga said, "We can see that."

The sheet shot away, and William gripped the ladder rung so it didn't take him with it. The tip of a sword appeared just inches from his face. His entire body sagged. "Shit!"

CHAPTER 17

"Climb out of there slowly." The woman stood with the sun at her back, its glare dazzling. She raised her voice at William's friends. "All of you need to come out slowly or I'll cut his eyes out before he has a chance to even consider running."

When none of them replied, the woman yelled, "You hear me?" As she forced her words out, she jolted forward and nicked William's cheek with the tip of her sword. It left a buzzing sting followed by the warm trickle of blood.

A chorus of dull voices, all but Artan replied, "Yes."

"And I know there's four more of you down there, so don't try to mug me off."

Directed by the woman's weapon, William climbed from the hole and stood to attention. The sun no longer in his eyes, he now recognised the short woman from inside the fortress. The angry horn blower with the two tattoos around her neck, her thick monobrow still fixed in a hard scowl. The spiteful little thing emanated malice.

The woman's long hair then shot to the side with a blow against the back of her head. A thick bar of wood. *Tonk!* Her eyes rolled and her legs buckled. *Clang!* Her sword hit the ground before falling into the hole William had just climbed from.

Olga shouted, "Steady on. We're coming up."

"Am I glad to see you," William said to a smiling Samson. And then he called into the hole, "It's okay, Olga. Samson just knocked her out and she dropped her sword. Someone can keep that as a weapon. Come up slowly; we're safe."

Samson clamped a hug around William that squeezed the air from his lungs and cracked his back. The large man kissed the top of his head before stepping away, a wide beaming grin dominating his face. "Am I glad to see you're okay."

Olga was the next one out of the hole, Max close behind, before William said, "How did you know we'd be here?"

"We saw you go in, and I convinced Missy to wait for you to come back out again. That way I knew it wouldn't get back to the community and I could help you."

Her hands on her hips, Olga stepped close to Samson and looked him up and down. "Why do you keep on helping us?"

"You've seen what they do in there."

Max looked at the wooden fence close by while Artan crawled from the hole with Missy's sword in his grip. Olga and William remained fixed on Samson.

"I can't do much when the whole community are against me, but when I'm out here, it's different. Besides, I don't want to stay here. Where are you going?"

Matilda emerged as the last of them while William pulled the scrunched-up map from his back pocket. He unfolded it to reveal their intended destination: the small community outside the ruins. He gave his friends a moment to object. "We're going here."

"What's there?"

"We think another community. We can't stay out in the wild forever. And anywhere's got to be better than Edin, right?"

Samson raised his eyebrows.

"Okay, maybe there are worse places, but chances are we can find somewhere better."

"And you think this is the place?"

"We hope it is," Olga said.

A usually confident man, Samson's shoulders hunched and he dropped his attention to his feet. "Do you have room in your party for one more?"

"I get the impression very few people are loyal to Magma and want to be in that place?" William said.

Samson paused and turned his head to one side. "There's a handful of fanatics, but not many."

"Do you know Trent?"

"Yeah. I'd count him in the few."

"He has a friend. A short black kid who was sent out hunting earlier today."

"Cyrus."

"If you say so."

"Yeah, it's Cyrus."

"We owe him. He let us through in the national service area when Edin fell, and I promised I'd be back for him."

"So you want me to bring him with me?"

"Can you?" William said. Then he checked the others. "Unless anyone objects?"

Of all of them, Artan's face twisted. But the glaze remained in the boy's eyes. He could have been thinking about something entirely different.

"I can get him out of the community. I'll take him hunting with me and we won't come back. Where shall we meet you and when?"

A large and twisted metal structure sat just over a hill in the direction of the new community. A skeleton of steel, the top ten feet or so visible, it was much more hidden behind the brow. The top had corroded with time. From the width of what remained, it had once been at least three times its current height. "That tower?" William said. "How about we meet you there in the morning?" The air had a slight bite to it from where the afternoon had grown long. "We all need a rest before we move on. We'll find somewhere to sleep and meet you there at first light. Sound good?"

Samson's familiar beaming smile returned and he clamped another tight hug on William before working through the others. When he got to Artan, the boy snarled, his fists balled, his shoulders pulled back.

"Thanks again," Samson said, eyeing Artan as he stepped away from him. "Can one of you hit me?"

Max's mouth fell open. "*What?*"

"Can one of you hit me? Missy didn't see who jumped her, so if I go back with a bruise, I can pretend we were blindsided while apprehending you."

"Um," William said. "I'm not sure—"

Crack! Olga landed a punch square on Samson's chin, his hair swinging as his head snapped away from the blow.

While holding his jaw, Samson opened and closed his mouth and laughed. "Wow! I won't be asking you to punch me again."

"If I punch you again"—Olga winked—"you won't get back up. That was me playing."

Samson laughed. He continued to hold his jaw as he walked off. "See you in the morning."

CHAPTER 18

Because Magma's community sat in a valley, they had to climb a hill to get away from it. Like with everywhere else in this decrepit city, the numerous ruins provided cover for their escape.

The hill's gradient stole the conversation from the group's lungs until Artan said, "I don't trust him."

Olga led the way while William dropped back to walk with Artan. "Who don't you trust?"

"Samson."

"Why?"

"I've just got a bad feeling."

"But he's helped us loads already. He helped us get to you in the political district. He's helped us get away from Magma's community. I'm not trying to be rude, but if you don't have any concrete reason other than a gut feeling, what do you expect or want us to do?"

The crack of Matilda's voice hit the back of William's neck like a snapping whip. "What do you want from him? He's got a bad feeling, so he's sharing that with you."

It took William a second to catch his breath after following

Olga and Max across a particularly wide gap back into hiding. He waited for Matilda and Artan to catch up. "I'm not trying to be disrespectful."

"Really?"

"Look, Matilda, I get you want to help him, and you want to make sure he has a voice, but I can't act on a bad feeling. Samson has helped us countless times, am I wrong?"

They shuffled sideways, their backs scraping against a long brick wall. Olga then led them through an old doorway, higher up the hill.

"Well?" William said.

"No."

"And it's not that I don't take Artan seriously. He's as important as everyone else in this group, and if he has a good reason not to trust Samson, I'm all ears. But we can't leave Samson and Cyrus stranded based on a hunch."

Both Olga and Max were slimmer than William. Olga naturally so, Max from his time in the labs' prison. So when Olga, and then Max, slipped through a gap in front of him, William paused. To go the long way around would make him visible to Magma's community. The chances of anyone watching were slim, but why risk it? They were nearly away from the horrible place. He turned sideways and pushed through the crack in the wall, clamping his jaw against the stone cutting into both his chest and back.

Matilda rejected William's hand when he reached out to help her through. When she and Artan caught up to them, he said, "Before we move, we need a plan. I don't want to be accused of not valuing anyone's opinion. So what do we do about Artan's feelings?"

"There!" Max pointed in the direction of the large metal structure, the top of it rusting and jagged from where it had once been taller.

William shrugged. "That's where we're going. So what?"

"Not the metal tower. *Next* to it. A little way away. See that church and spire?"

Not the tallest building over the hill, and they could only see the top of it, but the church remained standing and had a good line of sight to the metal tower. It had put up a valiant effort against the slow decay of time.

"Because it's not the biggest building around," Max said, "it's probably not the most obvious. We can hide out in it and get some rest. And we can see when Samson and Cyrus turn up—"

"So we'll be well hidden in case we see more of a reason not to trust them," Olga said.

When William looked at Artan, the boy offered nothing in response. "It does give us more time to decide." He turned to Matilda and raised his eyebrows. "Do you have a better plan than that?"

After she'd shared a look with Artan, Matilda shook her head. "No."

"Okay, Max, lead the way. Take us—"

The multitonal shriek from lower down the hill damn near shook dust from the buildings around them. Their line of sight blocked by the ruins, Olga hopped across several rocks to reach what had once been a first-storey window. "Shit."

Artan and Matilda went right, Max joined Olga on their left, and William peered through the gap they'd just squeezed through. A glimpse and then it vanished. Then another glimpse. Diseased flooded the ruins, swarming through the downed buildings.

"There's hundreds of them," Olga said. "I suppose it had to happen sooner or later. With the cage empty they had to get bored."

"They might not be chasing us," William said.

Olga again. "Does it matter? They're heading this way. If they're not chasing us now, they will be when they see us."

Matilda pulled back from the end of the wall. "You reckon we can get to that building in time, Max?"

The boy nodded. "If we go now."

If they had a better option, no one offered it. The others waited as if they wanted William's approval. He shooed Max away with his hands. "Go, Max. Go."

CHAPTER 19

William tried to find his rhythm, his legs burning as he powered up the hill.

Max might have picked their destination, but Olga took the lead. The girl crossed the landscape like a squirrel through trees, leaping from one lump of rock to the next, unerring in her judgement.

After bursting through another doorway and out into what had once been an old road, William waited.

When Matilda and Artan appeared, Matilda's face reddened. "What the hell are you doing?"

William took up the rear, the scream of the unseen diseased calling through the ruined city.

Still about one hundred feet from cresting the hill, William tugged on walls, rocks, and the metal bars to help pull himself forward. The rough scenery tore at his palms, his hands alive with the electric buzz of hundreds of small cuts. He ducked through another doorway, sidestepped a large crack in the ground, and hopped over a rock. Heaving heavy breaths, his legs turned weak as the others opened up a lead on him. He lost sight of them for seconds at a time in the ruined maze.

William skirted around a wall and ducked at the last moment, avoiding a metal bar destined to gouge out his left eye. He scraped his shin on another bar and yelled through clenched teeth. The pack behind grew louder; a plague on his heels. Their cacophony bad enough, whatever else he did, he shouldn't look back.

Olga vanished over the hill, Max next. Artan followed. Matilda stopped, waiting, her mouth wide from her heavy breaths, her face flushed. Her attention down the hill behind him, she winced and bounced on the spot, willing him to run faster. Anyone else and he might not have seen her urgency, but he knew Matilda too well. Her panic accelerated his already overworked heart.

William reached the top, Matilda turning to run as he got to her. *Don't look back. Don't look back.*

A slight decline, William's feet slipped on the bricks, rocks, and dust. Matilda flew over the environment ahead of him. Olga, Max, and Artan had already reached the ruined building Max had earmarked for their safety.

The wind at their backs, the collective reek of the diseased caught up to William.

Don't look back.

The rattling breaths of the front runners gained on him.

Don't look back.

William's lungs couldn't provide the oxygen he needed. The building about thirty feet away, Matilda reached it and climbed up.

Don't look back.

William looked back.

The diseased were everywhere and just feet away. He wouldn't make it. A wobble snapped through his tired legs, threatening to throw him to the ground.

They screamed as if they knew they'd won.

The wall of a building on his left, it stood at least ten feet tall. A window halfway up, he ran for it, jumped, and used the frame as a launch pad to climb to the top.

The front-running diseased crashed into the wall, shaking the structure as he climbed just out of their reach.

The beasts screamed and threw angry fists against the brickwork. They gnashed their yellow and black teeth.

William reached the top and sat down, panting. He might be safe for now, and their efforts to knock the structure down might never yield fruit, but he'd just climbed on top of a wall. Nothing more. The building it had once been no longer existed. At only two feet wide, it gave him nowhere to hide from their sight. If it came down to a battle of wills, he stood no chance. The diseased would wait for him forever.

At least twenty feet away from the old building where his friends waited, William took a moment to catch his breath. Sure, he had a chance to fill his lungs, but better respiration would do little against the sea of diseased just a few feet below him.

CHAPTER 20

The day wore on, the sky darkening with the onset of night. Dressed in a thin shirt, which had turned damp with his sweat, William hugged himself for warmth. A sea of ravenous diseased between him and his friends, they held him in their spotlight of crimson desire, their jaws working as if they could will him to fall with their insatiable hunger.

Dripping with shame, William avoided eye contact with Matilda. She glared at him from inside the church's roof and paced like a caged animal. He'd let her go first and now he'd ended up in possibly the most useless spot in the city: perched on a wall in plain sight, ensuring the crowd didn't disperse.

The others had made it to the church. It still had more than half its roof remaining. A wide structure only one storey tall, its spire stretched beyond that and also remained intact.

Max then took Missy's sword from Artan and slipped down through the gap in the roof while the others remained in the shadows. They had an evening and night to wait out, which would be plenty of time for the rancid freaks to piss off, were it not for William remaining in plain sight.

It didn't matter how many times he'd witnessed it, when

Max walked among the diseased, William's heart pounded in his throat. What if the rules changed and one of them bit him? Could his invulnerability wear off? Did it work with *every* diseased on the planet?

Not only did the creatures pay Max no mind, but he also had to shove and elbow his way through them to make a path to the wall William perched on. The rancid and acidic curdling of flesh damn near smothered William several feet above. God only knew what it was like for Max so close to them, although his twisting face and occasional heave gave some indication. And not only the stench, but many of the creatures had glistening patches of tacky and open wounds. Maybe the milky sludge offered lubrication through some of the tighter parts of the mob.

Max took a diversion, heading for a building close by. A tall metal pole, about eight feet long, hollow in the middle, and made from thick black metal clung to its side. He wriggled it free, the rusty clamps squeaking before the bricks gave them up with a small cloud of dust.

When Max tapped the pole against a nearby wall, the hollow tube rang like a bell and rust poured from it like sand. One tap, two taps, he then brought it down on the head of a diseased close by. Tap, tap, crunch. Just to be sure, he did it again, playing a basic rhythm on the landscape. Tap, tap, crunch.

Obviously strong enough, William took the pole Max offered up to him. The end glistened with the blood of Max's victims. After turning it around and holding the dry end, he used his elevated position to drive the pole down like a spear, stabbing it into the diseased's faces below. "Uh, Max," he said, "while I appreciate the help, this could take a while."

"I brought it so you can bridge the gap to that building."

A six-foot gap between William and the neighbouring ruins,

the pole would certainly bridge it, but ... "There's no way I can walk across this pole."

"No," Max said, "but you can hang beneath it and shimmy across."

William opened his mouth to argue, but he had nothing. The fact remained; if he and his friends were to move on, he needed to get out of sight like the rest of them. In his current spot he'd continue to attract more diseased, making their escape an impossibility. Were it not for him, they'd all be resting up in the church's loft by now.

William dropped into a crouch, shaking as he took the weight of leaning the pole across the gap between him and the next closest building. The pop of grit ran along its shaft as it nestled into a nook in a crumbling brick on the other side.

After he'd pressed on it with his weight, William found Max in the crowd. The only face he didn't mind looking up at him. "You'd best catch me if I fall."

Max laughed.

"Not helping!"

"Neither's talking about it. Get a move on, yeah? These things might not bite me, but that doesn't mean I want to spend the evening hanging out with them. They stink!"

The hard pole hurt William's chest when he lay across it, his entire weight against the metal makeshift bridge. He shimmied out, his fingers interlinked and his feet crossed at the ankles. He screamed when he spun around, now hanging over the creatures. Their shrill excitement drilled into his ears.

"Just don't look down," Max said.

"Stop talking to me and I won't!" William fixed on his destination, his palms sweating, his face twisted against the diseased's stink.

The structure on the other side as impractical a hiding place as the one he'd come from, but at least it took him closer to his friends. A long wall about eight feet from the ground and this one only a foot wide at the most. Wide enough to walk across as long as he didn't look down.

William's legs hung down when he transitioned from the pole to the wall. A diseased hand batted his foot before he snapped it away. He scrambled up and dragged the pole towards him. The end farthest away fell into the crowd with a *tonk!* It knocked a diseased to the ground. Those around it filled the gap instantly.

The diseased jostled and shoved around the base of the wall. William stabbed several of them in the face with the hollow pole.

"What are you doing?" Max said.

While clamping his jaw, William sank the pole into another diseased's nose. "It's making me feel better, okay? Let me have some power over them."

The gap to the next building stretched wider than the one he'd just crossed. He shook like before as he leaned the heavy pole across the space. He had it almost horizontal, fire streaking across his shoulders and twisting through his back. The end of the pole weaved, hovering in mid-air. It taunted him. Close to the wall, but not close enough.

William's arms gave out and he let the pole fall. It missed and scraped the wall on its way down, its momentum pulling him forwards. He let it drop so it didn't take him with it.

"Come on, William," Matilda called over to him. She clapped her hands once with a sharp *crack*. "You can do this!"

After Max retrieved the pole, his mouth moved, but the rowdy diseased drowned him out. William took the weaving end of the hollow metal tube when Max held it out to him, and waited while his friend kept a hold of the other side, lifting it above his head as he walked all the way to the other end.

The wall opposite had been constructed from large grey

rocks. Max found a place to step up and rest the end of the pole on the top. While he held it there, William did the same with his end, and Max tested it for him by hanging down from it. The pole stretched just a few inches longer than the gap. It would have to do. Overthink it, and he wouldn't make the journey.

As William fell around the pole, yelling for a second time while he hung down, he shook his head to himself.

Halfway across, the pole shifted with a *clunk!* William searched the wall on the other side. "What just happened, Max?"

The diseased clearly sensed his fear, those closest stretching an extra few inches as if they could reach him.

"You're doing fine."

As soon as the words left Max's mouth, the pole shifted again. *Clunk!* "Doesn't feel like I'm doing fine."

"Trust me, you're okay. But you might want to hurry up."

The pole dropped by half an inch. The diseased screamed louder. Their patience would pay off.

William quickened his pace, hand over hand, dragging his locked feet along the rough pole.

At the wall, William pulled himself on until he lay across the grey rocks. The rock they'd rested the pole on had a spider's web of cracks running through it. William tapped it and the grey lump shattered, turning to shrapnel. The pole fell into the diseased with the miniature landslide.

William paused for a moment to settle before he took the pole from Max again.

He crossed to the next building without incident. Its walls remained intact. Rectangular and about fifteen feet in length by eight feet wide, the short back wall stood strong while its opposite end had collapsed where the door frame had once been. William walked along to the back wall, holding the pole horizontally like a tightrope walker.

"You need to bring as many diseased into the building as possible, or around this side at least," Max said.

"What are you planning?"

"We're not far from safety."

"As the crow flies," William said. "The problem is, I'm not a crow."

"And there aren't any more buildings to cross to," Max said. "I'm going to set up stepping stones between here and our hide-out. There are enough rocks around."

"I'm not trying to cross a bog. The diseased will rip me off stepping stones in a heartbeat."

"Which is why you need to drag them back over here. Bait them so when you run, you can get ahead of them."

"Are you insane?"

"How about while I set it up, you see if you can think of a better solution?"

CHAPTER 21

I t took Max about ten minutes to set up the path he expected William to cross. In that time, William still hadn't come up with a better plan. The inaction had invited the cold back into his bones. The sky had turned gunmetal grey with the onset of night. They were running out of time.

Six large stones in total, each one no more than four feet tall. The largest gap between them stretched three feet at the most. It took William back to the wooden platforms they'd hopped across while they trained prior to their time extending Edin's wall. The jumps before him were much easier. Although, if he fell here, he'd lose more than his pride.

"I can't do it." William stood up as if it would help him better assess the path he had to take and shook his head again. "I can't do it."

"Go to the back corner of the building and drag the diseased with you," Max said. "It'll clear the way. I'll track you from the ground."

"There must be another option."

"Until you're out of sight, we're screwed."

Matilda, Artan, and Olga watched William from the church's attic. When he got there, he could rest for the night. But he had to get there first. He laughed. "You think I can make this jump, Tilly?"

She cupped her mouth with both hands to be heard over the diseased. "Of course. You can make any jump."

"But you always said—"

"I was winding you up. Come on, you can do this. Don't overthink it."

The words lifted William and he filled his chest with a deep breath. He stood an inch or two taller. He *could* do this.

William's legs trembled as he walked along the back wall to the far corner of the old building. Many diseased piled in through the once door, many more surged around the outside, all of them fighting to gather around him.

Max moved far enough away from the building to allow William to see him from his current spot. When he gave William a thumbs up, William filled his lungs one more time and stepped forwards. But his legs turned weak and he shook his head.

"Come on, William," Max said. "You can do this."

Several nods to himself, William then took off. The top of the building uneven, his feet twisted and turned to accommodate the awkward angles as he tore across the short back wall, turned to run across the long wall, and when he reached the end, jumped for the first rock. What if Max hadn't settled it properly?

Too late now. The rush of diseased behind him, Max running at his side, William returned to his training in national service, to following the trail blazed by Matilda on the wet poles. One step on each stone, he landed on the first one and propelled himself towards the next.

The gaps between each were easy enough to cross. Five stones to go, four, three—

A diseased slashed at his feet, clipping him as he leaped, but unable to hold on. William landed on the penultimate stone off-balance, the large rock wobbling beneath his step.

Another diseased in front of him, it waited to trip him on the next stone.

Max body-checked the creature aside, and William jumped as if driven forward by the diseased's roar crashing into his back like a strong wave.

William kicked off the last stone, the final leap to the building with his friends in. He caught the edge, his lower body slamming against the stone wall.

Matilda, Artan, and Olga grabbed William's arms and the back of his shirt, tearing cuts along his front as they dragged him up over the rough bricks and into the attic with them.

Breathless, William rolled over onto his back and stared up through the gap in the roof at the dark sky. He laughed. It started as a giggle, but he soon lost control. Matilda leaned down and planted a kiss against his forehead while he covered his eyes to hide his tears.

When Max appeared a few seconds later, William stood on shaking legs. "Thanks, man."

"Anytime. You okay?"

"I will be." He hugged Max, pulling away instantly. "Jeez, you stink!"

Max shook his head. "Funny that!"

"Let me do the first watch," Artan said, taking the sword from Max.

Although Matilda opened her mouth to object, Artan said, "Don't worry; I'm fine. I could do with the time on my own."

"You sur—?"

"Yes."

Wᴵʟʟᴵᴀᴍ ᴀɴᴅ Mᴀᴛᴵʟᴅᴀ ʟᴇᴀɴᴇᴅ ᴀɢᴀᴵɴꜱᴛ ᴛʜᴇ ʙᴀᴄᴋ ᴡᴀʟʟ, holding one another as night settled in. Max and Olga sat nearby, the shadows inside the church's roof almost hiding them from sight. They were close, but from the way Olga leaned towards him, not as close as she would have liked. The stench clearly didn't bother her.

The fading light turned Artan into a silhouette. Only a few feet away, he faced out in the direction of the large metal structure like a gargoyle on the edge of a Gothic building. The metal frame's base stretched at least fifteen feet by fifteen feet. Decay had bitten the top off. How much taller had it been in its heyday?

As she nestled into his hug, Matilda said, "What was that about earlier?"

"Which part?"

"The chivalrous bullshit part. Again!"

"Huh?"

"Like when you let me go first up the back ladder of the gym in the national service area."

"I told you, that was because you're the fastest climber. By going up first, you cleared the ladder for us quicker."

"Okay, let's say I believe that—and I'm not saying I do— how can you justify waiting for me back there? You think you're stronger and faster than me or Artan?"

"No."

"What, then?" Despite still leaning against him, Matilda's frame had tensed.

The words caught in William's throat.

"Come on, if it's not your male ego, what the hell is it?"

"I'm sorry. I see that I shouldn't have done it. The thing is, I care more about your life than I do my own."

Matilda relaxed. It took her a few seconds to say, "Oh." She leaned into him again.

William rested against the wall, held Matilda, and closed his eyes. Hopefully sleep would come, but even if it didn't, the rest and proximity to his love would be more than enough to get him through tomorrow.

CHAPTER 22

Pins and needles ran down William's right arm from where he'd spent the night hugging Matilda. The funky taste of morning lay along his tongue, and his clothes were damp and cold with dew. The black sky had turned dark blue on the horizon.

If anything, the gap between Olga and Max had grown wider. From the way Olga faced him, and from the way Max turned away, he'd initiated the distance between them. Artan—his back hunched as he hugged his knees to his chest—still sat close to the edge of the building, staring out over the ruined city.

While biting down on his bottom lip as if it would keep his actions slow and quiet, William twisted free from Matilda, laying her down on her side. Despite the chill, he removed his top, the early morning giving him gooseflesh as he lay his shirt across her sleeping form.

Close to the edge of the building, but far enough back to be hidden from sight, William sat beside Artan. The boy continued to study the horizon, his eyes bloodshot, heavy bags beneath them. The lack of sleep had turned his haunted, withdrawn face positively skeletal. "What do you think this city once looked like?"

For a moment, Artan remained dead still. Just before William could ask him again, he said, "Beautiful." Tears stood in his eyes.

The twisted and broken pylon close by, William squinted against the wind. "Still no Samson and Cyrus, then? Or anyone else for that matter? Why didn't you ask someone to switch with you? You look like you need the rest. Do you want to have a quick sleep now while I stay here?"

"I wouldn't have been able to sleep anyway," Artan said.

The main crowd might have moved on, but the diseased still meandered through the ruins. Some alone, some in pairs. One— a woman dressed in a stained pink nightie, torn and grey with dirt—stumbled through the rocks and fallen walls, her face a slack mask of shattered turmoil. She looked like a mother who'd lost a child. Yet, despite her plight, no one else gave a shit.

"What was it like in Edin? I didn't get to see most of it," Artan said.

"Awful. It fell so fast." William shuddered and clenched his jaw against his trembling body. "There were thousands of them. It was like every diseased within a ten-mile radius sensed the opening and charged into the city."

"And Hugh was the one who left the gate open?"

"Yeah." William sighed. "He left Edin to come and find us …" What would he achieve telling him Hugh busted out to let them know Artan was still alive? That Edin fell because of his need to deliver that specific message. If Matilda wanted to tell him, he wouldn't stop her, but it certainly wasn't his place to reveal it, and the boy didn't need it on his shoulders. Especially not at the moment. Max must have known why Hugh left too. Being the one who told Hugh about it in the first place. He finally filled the silence. "His head wasn't in the right place."

The two boys watched the horizon, a light blue band where the sky met the ground. William finally said, "But if it wasn't for Hugh, we wouldn't be here. He might have lost his head, but in the end, he fought like no one else I've seen."

"Why did he kill himself?"

The wind added to the burn from the rising sun. William blinked several times, his throat locking so tight it strained his words. "He said he was done. I hate to say it, but the truth is, he became a liability. I miss him every day, but he kept making mistakes. And if his mistakes had led to Matilda's death, I wouldn't have ever forgiven him. He screwed up a few times and put us in the firing line because of it." He flinched as images of Hugh getting dragged beneath the rush of diseased in the labs' corridor charged through his mind. "And as much as we would have stood by him and helped him, Hugh didn't want to be saved."

For as long as William wanted to talk, Artan listened. A lull in the conversation, the boy said, "I'm sorry about your mum and dad."

"Me too, mate. And yours."

"Mum wouldn't have lasted five minutes in this new world." Artan's expression turned stony. "And Dad had to go. I'd do it all over again."

"I've seen a lot of people die over the past few days. I even had to kill someone. When Olga and I were following you back to Magma's fortress, a woman jumped out. We would have been caught if I didn't take her down. There was nothing else I could do."

"Needs must," Artan said.

"Sure, but it's not an easy thing to take a life. And it must be harder when you've known that person like you knew your dad. No matter how justified or how much you hated them."

When Artan snapped alert, it took William a few seconds of scanning the horizon to see the tall figure with thick curly hair. A shorter person walked at his side.

"Before we wake the others," William said, "I want you to make this choice. I trust your instinct about Samson. Do we go to meet them or not?"

"My gut says no, but I don't think that's enough to condemn someone to death."

"I need to know you're happy with this, Artan."

The boy winced as he stood up and stretched. He then walked over to wake Matilda.

LIKE MOST THINGS IN THE RUINED ENVIRONMENT, THE TALL METAL structure wore its decay like a peeling layer of skin. A coating of rust on the twisted and pockmarked steel, the gritty flakes rubbing off on William's palms as he climbed. Unlike the building they'd spent the night in, the metal skeleton had few places to hide from the sight of the diseased. Although Samson and Cyrus watched him, he kept his words back until he'd climbed close to them.

"First," William said to Cyrus, holding out his hand to shake, "I want to introduce myself. I'm William, and I told you I'd be back."

Cyrus' smile lit his face as he accepted William's gesture, his grip firm. He laughed. "That you did."

Then William turned to Samson. "Thank you for meeting us here. Can we move somewhere else?" Even as he spoke, Matilda, Artan, Olga, and Max fought on the ground, taking down the diseased who appeared beneath them. He'd left his sword with Matilda. "We need to be somewhere where we can hide from the diseased."

THEY CHOSE A BUILDING TOWARDS THE EDGE OF THE RUINED city and climbed onto its roof. Only one storey high and half of it had already collapsed. The other half looked like it would soon follow. Samson had brought a sack with him, and now they were sitting again, he handed out water, carrots, bread, and some dried meat.

"This ain't human, is it?" Olga said, eyeing the cured brown strip. "Coming from Magma's fortress and all."

Samson laughed. "Protein is protein."

"This *is* human?"

He laughed again and shook his head. "Don't worry, Magma hasn't got that desperate yet."

"Yet?" Olga said.

"Come on, you saw what he was like. If the animal meat ever runs out, he won't think twice."

Resisting the urge to drain his flask of water in one, William took slow sips in between mouthfuls of deer. Too much and he'd throw it all back up again or, at the very least, spend the next few hours trying not to.

Several diseased's cries, Samson leaned forward to watch a small pack of the vile things pass through the ruins below them. "This place is a nightmare."

"You have no idea," William said, his shoulders still sore from dragging himself along the pipe over the crowd of creatures the previous day.

"You think?" Samson lost focus. "Remember the one hundred that left the arena? I was the only one who survived."

"Sorry, of course you have an idea. I was more referring to yesterday; there were hundreds of them. If Max—"

"Hadn't found that old building to hide in," Olga said and her eyes narrowed, "we would have been screwed."

Not only did Olga glare at him, but Max, Matilda, and Artan all stared his way too. And rightly so. He'd nearly outed the boy when he'd specifically asked them not to. It didn't matter if he trusted Samson and Cyrus, Max had to be the one to tell them.

"I'm sorry we left you on the roof in the national service area," William said.

Cyrus shrugged. "It's fine. I get it. I didn't want to go into Edin anyway. You said you'd be back, and you were true to your word."

"If only Trent saw it that way."

"Trent's better off with Magma. They're on the same wavelength."

William pulled the map from his pocket again and stretched it out on the roof. The small blue blob of the nearest community sat close to the edge of the ruins. They were already at the city's border, the old buildings giving way to grass, rocks, and fallen walls scattered throughout the lush expanse. His finger on the community, William said, "I don't think we're very far away from this place."

"That's the plan, is it?" Samson said. "Find another community to settle in?"

"You have a better one?" William said.

After a moment, his thick jaw working on the piece of bread he'd just bitten off, Samson shrugged. "No. I think the safety of being inside walls makes sense. There's no future in living on roofs, scavenging as we move from elevated position to elevated position." He pointed out across the grasslands. "From the look of the map, I think we should head that way."

When no one else offered any thoughts, William folded the map. "Shall we move on, then?"

OLGA HAD TRIED TO HOLD MAX'S HAND, BUT HE'D PULLED away. Instead, she strode ahead of the group, walking backwards through the long dewy grass, her hands hanging down as she dragged them through the meadow. She faced her friends and what they were leaving behind. "I suppose this is it, then? We had somewhere to hide when we ran into the diseased in the ruins." She drew her sword and spun full circle, her eyes aglow. "We see any now and we have to stand and fight."

By the time William had drawn breath to warn her, Olga had backed into the tip of the boy's spear. She stopped and turned around. The boy lifted the flint point to her face, his thick arms holding the shaft with a tight grip. Fifteen to twenty of them—all boys around William's age and older—appeared from the long grass. Naked from the waist up, they were all ripped. Fit lads. Hunters. Each of the boys was armed with a spear. Each one decorated with what looked like the dried blood of their prey. Each one had their hair shaved to the scalp. They were warriors unlike any he'd seen before, and they were in charge of the situation.

The largest of all of them was a boy maybe two to three years older than William. His closely cropped hair revealed a hint of red, the same flecks in his stubble. Eyes of deep hazel, he spoke with a measured calm. "Put your weapons down, and we won't hurt you."

Olga let her sword go, and before William could hand his over, someone behind him pulled it from its sheath and discarded it nearby.

Artan glared at Samson while throwing his sword to the ground. "*You* set this up!"

The tip of a spear resting against the back of his skull, Samson shrugged. "What the hell are you talking about?"

"You set us up. You've handed us to Magma on a plate."

"Who the hell's Magma?" the lead hunter said. "You know what? Don't answer that. The next one to speak will get a spear through the back of their head. I don't know how you've survived out here; you walk through the grass like cattle. If you want to stay alive, shut up and come with us."

The spear tip pressed against the base of William's skull stung like an ant's bite. One hard lunge would force the flint through the front of his face. He moved off with the others, a million questions silenced by the threat of death.

CHAPTER 23

T he boys with the spears dictated their pace, a slow trudge through the long grass. William could do slow; although, the longer they took to get wherever they were heading, the longer it would be before they discovered their fate.

The dew in the long grass turned William's trousers cold and heavy with damp. The fabric rubbed against his thighs.

Every time William turned to look at one of the others, the sharp sting of a spear tip jabbed into the back of his neck, and the hunter behind him hissed. He'd managed one or two shared looks with Matilda, and her face told him everything he needed to know. Outnumbered and weaponless, they had no chance against these hunters. Not yet at least.

The spear tip pressed against William's neck again. He spun away from it, turning to the hunter behind him. Several more spears shot up, an array of tips now inches from his face. His heart quickened. "Look, we're doing what you want us to. I get you can kill me should you feel the need, so how about you ease up a little, yeah? We'd be mad to try anything stupid."

The hunter's bright blue eyes shone and he bared his teeth, hissing at William again. A shaved head and topless like the rest of his crew, he had deep purple scars around his neck as if someone had made several attempts to behead him. Although he continued to glare at William and his expression remained unchanged, he showed the slightest concession by pulling his spear back.

A hand clamped on William's right shoulder. He jumped and spun around. The leader of the pack, the boy with streaks of red in his hair and stubble, smiled. His hazel eyes remained cold and sharp. Intelligent and calculating.

"I'm William," William said.

The hunter dipped a nod. "Slate."

"Pleased to meet you." What the hell was he doing? Pleased to meet you? The hunters were one step away from slaughtering them. "Although—" William scoffed a laugh "—it would have been nice to meet you in different circumstances. Now we've finally introduced ourselves, can you tell me what you're planning to do with us?"

Slate squinted against the wind. He gripped his spear with both hands before turning his back on William and scanning the meadow ahead. "We'd rather not kill you, if that's what you mean. We're going to take you to our community and look after you."

"Look after?"

"There's no subtext there, William. We genuinely mean you no harm."

"Then forgive me for asking, but if you mean us no harm, why are you holding us hostage?"

"We're as cautious of you as you are of us. It's a wild world. I'd call it a healthy suspicion. Let's use this time to get to know one another and not do anything stupid, yeah? Sudden movements like the one you just pulled make us jumpy."

"We don't want to fight you," William said.

"Look, kid, we don't know that."

Kid? William clenched his jaw. Slate couldn't have been any more than two years older than him at the most. "But why get us to drop our weapons? Why didn't you just take them from us?"

"Swords are crass and clumsy."

"They've done right by us so far."

"They didn't stop you getting ambushed, did they?" Slate then pointed in the direction they were heading with the tip of his spear. He raised the end of it to his right eye and looked down its shaft as if to assess its straightness. "Why use a sword when you have something as graceful as this? Also, how many deer have you taken down with a blade?"

Led by Slate, they set off again. The hunters without prisoners marched like an army. Straight backed, stepping in time, they also scanned their surroundings. They were ready for war. And a good job too.

The long grass swished as the creatures tore through it. Despite their screams, rattling breaths, and clumsy steps, the overgrown meadow hid them from sight.

The hunters turned their backs to William and his friends and formed a ring around them, their spears pointing out. Three of them remained inside the ring, guarding their prisoners.

When Max looked at him, William raised his eyebrows. Could he get them out of this somehow? They'd have his back if he made a move.

The hunter who'd shepherded William with his spear launched his attack. Propelled by his thick and bulging arms, his shot landed true, slamming into the creature's face, the tip bursting out through the back of its head.

The rest of the mob appeared. They were about fifteen feet away. Ten spears, maybe more, launched from all around them. Every attack landed, dropping the creatures as they ran.

Before the diseased got to within arm's length, they were all wiped out. Half the hunters still held onto their weapons, including Slate. Those who'd already thrown theirs had another one strapped to their back, which they were yet to draw.

The hunters cleaned their weapons on the wet grass while Slate turned to his prisoners. He maintained his two-handed grip on his spear. "See, it can be used both up close and from a distance." It took for him to pull the long knife with a curved blade from his belt for William to see they all had them. "And if they get too close, which they rarely do, we have these."

"What about the other spear?" William said. "Why didn't any of the hunters draw the extra one?"

"That's for hunting game. We try to keep them free of diseased blood."

Before the attack, the hunters had been stoic. Now they'd sated their lust for destruction, their frames were more relaxed, and several of them even smiled as they rejoined the group—all except the one with the scars around his neck. If anything, he frowned harder than before and shoulder barged William as he passed him.

Slate led them away. "Look," he said, "we really want this to work out. Experience has taught us to be cautious of other people, and for the sake of us and our community, we will maintain that caution. But we always want things to go smoothly. We'd rather make friends than enemies. I'm sure you understand."

William didn't want to speak for the group, but none of them appeared to want to speak for themselves—not even Olga, and for as long as he had known her, she'd always had something to say. "We understand," he finally said. "Now where are you taking us?"

They crested a small hill, the landscape opening up in front of them, and the long grass swayed in the wind. A large stone structure stood in the distance. The remains of an old castle, it had been repurposed to be the front of a community, the rest of the space penned in with wooden fencing similar to the one around Magma's fortress—too similar, in fact. Thick wooden stakes the size of tree trunks, sharpened to enough of a point to send a message. The community they'd seen on the map. "This is where we were heading," William said. "Is this where you're from?"

"Why were you heading for us?"

"We want to find somewhere else to live. We came from Edin on the other side of the ruins. The gates were left open and the place fell." William's cheeks burned under the intensity of Olga's glare.

"Well, let's hope this works out."

Maybe William imagined the way Slate glanced at Matilda. What plans did he have for her? For him and her? No, he'd imagined it. He couldn't let his paranoia take over.

"We're always looking for useful members for our little society. Can you hunt, kid?"

And there it goes again. Kid!

"I reckon I can," Olga said.

Although Slate maintained a straight face, several of the hunters snorted laughs at Olga's suggestion.

"What?" she said.

"Women don't hunt in our community," Slate said.

"You worried they'll show you up?"

It had to be more than paranoia. Slate definitely directed his reply at Matilda. "We believe in looking after our women. They're too valuable to us to send into the wild lands."

"That's one way to look at it," Olga said. "Another word for it is *oppression*."

William's heart sank. They were so close to the community. If she didn't wind her neck in, it could all go to shit. Thankfully, Slate didn't reply, and thankfully, Olga let it slide.

"What about you, kid?" Slate said.

"*William.*"

"Huh?"

"My name's William."

"Whatever. What really matters is are you any good with a spear?"

"Yeah. I am."

Matilda's eyes widened. Hopefully, the hunters missed it. He'd never used a spear in his life, but what else could he say to the jumped-up prick? He'd been eyeing his girl, calling him kid, and his gang still had them at spear point. Other than his honeyed words, everything about this group emanated hostility. But at least they were still alive. And until the gang proved otherwise, they had to take them at their word.

Slate smiled. "Good. We need more hunters."

"Good." At some point, William would have to back up his claim.

CHAPTER 24

As they drew closer to the fort, the hunters finally lowered their spears. They were clearly still ready to use them, but at least they showed William and the others some respect by allowing them to walk their own path. Maybe they had made the right choice in seeking out this community after all.

Unlike the others, Slate slid his spear into the holder on his back—tip down so it didn't contaminate the deer-hunting spear. While walking backwards in front of the group, he spread his arms wide. "Welcome to Umbriel. It's not much, but it's home. I'm not an historian, but it doesn't take a genius to see this place used to be a castle."

The hunter to William's left had his spear just in reach. If he moved fast enough, he could disarm him and attack. But where would that get them? They'd be overwhelmed in seconds.

The old castle had been built from large grey rocks, each one at least two feet square. The windows were small slits no more than six inches wide. The heads of what looked like children ran along the walkway, visible as they flashed past the lower parts of the toothy design topping the wall. Like many of the buildings from a lost world, some of the castle had collapsed, the right side considerably lower than the left. Large grey rocks littered the landscape, nestled in amongst the long grass.

"Our elders made the gates under the instruction of Grandfather Jacks," Slate said. "And we built the wooden wall out the back. It's proven to be a good front to Umbriel. It keeps the diseased at bay." He then led them down a short and steep slope. "This used to be what's called a moat. Filled with water, it made it hard for any attackers to get into the castle. We thought about refilling it, but what we already have is enough to protect against the diseased."

The thunderous rattle of chains made William jump and sent his pulse racing. The gate slowly lifted.

The pack of hunters closed in to walk through the castle's narrow entrance. William rubbed shoulders with Samson and Matilda, nodding at his love, who, although pale, returned a tight-lipped smile. Several spears close enough to grab, Slate dragged William's attention away when he said, "You'll love Umbriel, and the people will love you. We hope you like it here. We could always do with growing our community. Especially if the new members are young and fit."

Slate aimed the last comment at Matilda. Heat flushed William's cheeks and he balled his fists. When Cyrus looked down at them, he let his hands fall open again. Maybe Slate needed to know William and Matilda were a thing. After all, he couldn't blame him for finding her attractive, and he didn't want to risk their lives because of his jealousy.

When the gate had lifted high enough, Slate led them up the other side of the moat and in through the entrance.

The children on the top of the castle had been giggling and shrieking as they ran from one end to the other. Giddy pups waiting to see what had come to their home. A child's scream then cut through the mirth. It turned William's blood to ice, and before he had a chance to react, Slate slammed into him, driving him aside as one of the huge grey rocks fell from the top of the castle and landed where William had stood just seconds ago.

Pinned to the ground by the lead hunter, William squirmed but couldn't get free. When Slate got off him, he held his hand down to help him up. "Are you okay?"

The rock had landed on its end, half buried in the damp ground. "That would have crushed me."

While waving a clenched fist in the air, Slate yelled, "If I find out who knocked that rock off, you'll be getting kicked out of this community. Of course," he said to William with a shrug, "none of them will rat another one out, but I needed to threaten them. Kids, eh?"

His pulse quickening as his adrenaline finally caught up with him, William raised his eyebrows at Matilda. That was too close.

Once they'd entered Umbriel, the chains rattled again and the large gate lowered behind them. Matilda moved close to William and held his hand. "You okay?"

"I think so."

A group of kids rushed over to greet their new visitors. From two-year-olds to teenagers, they ran around William and the others. Wide eyes and broad smiles, one of them poked William, giggled, and ran away.

"Shoo!" Slate said, but it took for him to draw his spear before they scattered, cackling as they went. "Sorry. They don't get out, so it's super exciting for them when someone new comes to visit."

"Do you get many new people here?" Max said.

"There aren't many travellers this far north."

"So what's in the south—?"

But before William finished, Olga said, "You like to keep

your women in check, eh? This place is quite the picture of domesticity."

Maybe two hundred people in front of them, at least a third of them women. They were cleaning or cooking, busying themselves while a gaggle of men sat around. No doubt they'd been relaxing and chatting before William and the others had arrived.

If Slate heard Olga's comment, he let it slide. Max spoke under his breath. "Now's not the time for that. Remember, you don't change anything by shouting at people."

"What about cutting their throats?" Olga said.

Again, Slate did well to ignore it, his only concession to explain the place better. "Those men over there were once hunters. We like to retire them at twenty-five. From sixteen to twenty-five, they provide the meat to Umbriel. After that, they've earned their rest."

"What about the women?" Matilda said this time. "When do they earn their rest?"

Again, Slate ignored the accusation.

The fence—although similar to the one around Magma's fortress—penned in a space twice as large as the ex-protectors' home. Were the spikes on the top for anything other than effect? Had any diseased ever climbed walls? Although maybe they weren't spiked to keep things out. Maybe it was much more about keeping people in.

A field took up about a quarter of the space over in the far left corner. William nodded in its direction. "What do you grow here? Wheat?"

"Yeah." Slate nodded.

"I'm guessing you've just sown the seeds for this season's crop. That's hard graft."

"Tell me about it. We could have done with meeting you lot a few weeks ago."

The back wall of the community had wooden scaffolding

along it much like the back wall of Edin. William's throat stung and his eyes burned. How he'd loved those times with his dad.

A large wooden hut stood in the centre of the place. Just large enough to accommodate those there. They must have used it more in the winter. A fire burned out the front near where all the retired hunters sat. A stew bubbled in a large pot.

A dusty rectangle of space in front of the fire, a game of some sort. It had been marked out with a small trench around the outside and had three wooden hoops at either end in the shape of a pyramid, the two at the bottom wider than the one at the top.

Now they'd had time to take the place in, Slate brought his large hands together with a loud clap. "People of Umbriel, I'd like you to welcome our guests. We hope they might become residents. I want you to give them a hunter's welcome."

A deep baseline beat heralded the arrival of several teenagers. Girls and boys, they appeared with large wooden drums strapped to them as they hammered out a tribal rhythm. Many of the women and children screamed and yelled, some of them rolling their tongues as they all descended on the dusty rectangle in the middle of the community.

Clouds kicked up from their feet when they danced. Even the retired hunters stood up. Many of them were still young, but the older ones moved with surprising fluidity. The groove cared not for age and frailty.

To be the focus of the community's attention tightened William's lungs, his throat still burning for the loss of his father. Had Slate not mentioned the name, he might not have recognised it in the celebrations. Although, the people shouted it so frequently, how could he ignore the praise to Grandfather Jacks?

Both Olga and Matilda stood tense as if they were ready to fight. Max held himself more at ease, and Artan appeared unaffected by the celebrations. Cyrus stood close to Samson, the boy from national service as calm as Matilda's brother.

Several children ran forward, screaming and rolling their tongues. They brought offerings with them. They had flasks of water and strips of meat. Some of them had small loaves of bread. Wheat was clearly in shorter supply than whatever animal the meat belonged to. Maybe the hunters in this place had earned their retirement.

Slate leaned close to William and still had to shout to be heard. "If you're as good as you say you are with a spear, you'll be helping to deliver a ready supply of meat to this community. If you choose to stay, that is."

Why had William bragged about using a spear? What an idiot. He smiled and chewed on the salty meat before biting off a mouthful of the rough bread.

Several younger women came forwards. All locked into the same groove, they danced with more ferocity than the others, confident in their well-rehearsed routine. They stamped their feet and threw their hands in the air. When they were close, the women reached out for William, Artan, Max, Samson, and Cyrus, while Slate and the hunter with the scars on his neck took Matilda and Olga.

Max's cheeks glowed as the gruesome hunter led Olga away. No doubt William looked as bad watching Matilda. But what could they do? They were guests here. This was their ritual.

His body stiff, William danced like he had no control over his limbs.

The drumbeat then stopped and the community cleared from the dusty rectangle. A chair had been placed in the centre of the pitch.

"What's this for?" Samson said.

The only answer came in the form of his own echo.

The wind tossed the dust kicked up from the celebrations. It stuck to William's sweating skin. None of the others accepted the invitation of an empty chair until Matilda stepped forward. But a woman nearby gently grabbed her and shook her head. "Not for you, honey. It's for the men."

When none of the others moved, William sat in the chair.

A man with a machete approached. He wore a charcoal mask that made the whites of his eyes pop. Slate stood near Matilda.

"What's going on?" William said.

"Chill out, kid. Everything's under control." He stepped even closer to Matilda.

"You want to be a hunter," the man with the knife said, "you need to look like a hunter."

Every one of the hunting party had their hair shaved to the scalp. Maybe they hadn't committed to joining the community yet, but what harm would it do to have a haircut? God knew he needed it.

The barber, an older man in his thirties, leaned over William, blocking his escape. He lifted the knife to the side of his head.

William winced at the first cut, anticipating the burning nick of the blade biting into his flesh. But the experienced hair-dresser worked like the wind, removing chunks of his hair with sweeping cuts.

When the barber stepped away, William rubbed the stubble on his head and stood up to coos and giggles from the crowd. The wind chilled his scalp and his cheeks flushed until he met Matilda's gaze. She grinned at him. "It looks okay?"

She nodded.

The boys went one after the other. When Artan had finished, his lack of hair combined with his gaunt features to make him positively skeletal.

Samson shook his head. "No way. I'm too old to be a hunter anyway."

"All of the men need to do their time outside the walls," Slate said.

Although Samson drew a breath to reply, when he looked around, he clearly noticed the focus of the entire community on him. He shook his head and took his seat. For the entire time the barber cut his long curly hair, he glared at Slate.

The barber stepped away, leaving a bald Samson locked in his own seething fury while the people cleared the large rectangular space. William and his friends were the last to move.

Slate and four of his hunters moved to one end by the rectangle and stood in front of the three rings. Five other lads from the hunting party moved to the other end.

Two older women in their forties approached. One with curly blonde hair, and one with straight black hair. They were about the same age and the same height of around five feet and seven inches. But the similarities ended there. The one with black hair had blue eyes, the blonde one's eyes were brown. Both wore kind maternal smiles, the spreading of their grins twisting through William's chest. He'd never see his mum again. The blonde one had a fuller face than her friend and spoke first. "You're about to witness a game of tri-rings. This is Umbriel's favourite sport."

They led William and his friends to the side of the pitch.

"How many women play this game?" Olga said.

The black-haired woman laid a gentle hand on Olga's fore-arm. "Women don't play this game, sweetie."

"And you don't want to play?"

Both women shook their heads.

"Would they let you if you did?"

Both women shook their heads again.

Olga folded her arms across her chest, her scowl deepening. "That sounds like some kind of bullshit to me."

William chewed the inside of his mouth and watched his short friend. Everything could turn sour fast, because when Olga smelled bullshit, she wasn't very good at keeping her mouth shut.

CHAPTER 25

"Look, Olga," William said as they watched the teams loosen up for the match, "this isn't the time."

"Screw you!"

"I'm not saying you don't have a valid point." Slate's team consisted of what appeared to be him and the four fittest hunters. "You and Matilda have every right to be pissed. You're as much warriors as any of us."

"I'd say more so."

"I know you would, and I love you for that. My point is now's not the time."

"Are you trying to keep this little woman quiet?"

"Have you met Olga?"

When Olga frowned, William said, "Trying to keep you quiet is like trying to climb a greasy pole. I'm appealing to your common sense. Now's not the time for this. I support everything you're saying—"

"Just when it suits you."

"When it suits *all* of us. Speaking your mind isn't always a virtue, you know? Especially when the rest of us might have to pay the price for it."

Although Olga drew her breath to reply, Max reached across and placed a hand at the base of her back. Anyone else and she would have swung for them. The tension left her short frame and she melted into his touch, which he quickly withdrew.

William held Matilda's hand. "I'm with you on this, I really am. I won't stay in a place that pushes you and Olga down. I just think we need to pick our battles, and when to fight them."

Matilda acknowledged his gesture with an almost imperceptible nod, her dark eyes showing a will as fierce as Olga's. She'd fight when the time came.

The two older women wore wry smiles as they watched the debate. The lull in conversation prompted the blonde lady with the curly hair to move through the group and shake their hands one at a time. A warm and soft grip, she nodded at William. "I'm Rita, by the way, and this is Mary." The woman with the black hair smiled.

The blonde woman held Olga's hand for longer than the others. "It's going to be a pleasure to have you here, honey. You're exactly what this place needs."

Another round of beating drums, a group of four boys and four girls marched onto the tri-rings pitch, all of them hammering in time. The younger spectators on the sidelines danced and threw their hands in the air. A girl of about fourteen approached William and the others. She wore her brown hair in plaits tied around the top of her head like a crown. A wide grin showed off her brilliant white teeth. She shouted over the opening ceremony, the drums inciting the same tongue rolling and stamping William had quickly grown accustomed to with Umbriel. "I'm Dianna. Slate wanted me to come over and explain the game to you. It's called tri-rings. The rules are quite simple. You have two goals, each with three rings in. There's a small ball made from rope." She tossed a ball to William, who caught it.

"It's as hard as a rock," William said, squeezing it in his grip.

Dianna nodded. "You don't want to get hit by it. See those lines along the pitch?" A line ran the width of the pitch at each end. They sectioned off the final ten feet or so. "Those areas are for the defenders only. To score, the attackers of the opposing team have to throw the ball through one of the rings without crossing into the defensive areas. The two larger ones lower down"—the two bottom ones were both about two feet in diameter—"are worth one point each. The smaller one at the top"—about one foot in diameter—"is worth two. The winner is the first team to seven. Other than that, there are no rules. Whatever it takes to get the ball in the ring is fair game."

While the drummers made their way from the pitch, the teams still limbering up, Max nodded at the group of larger boys. "How often does Slate's side lose?"

"They never have. In fact, no one's even scored against them. They win every game seven nil."

The opposition team wore their fear with their hollow display of bravado. They jumped and leaped, stretched and twisted. The average age of the five boys was at least two years younger than that of Slate's team. They were children facing men in their prime. By comparison, Slate's team all stood dead still, staring at their opponents.

Dianna took the rope ball back from William before jogging onto the pitch and placing it inside a small centre circle drawn on the ground with chalk. She turned to the crowd. "Praise be to Grandfather Jacks and all he provides."

The crowd responded in unison, "To Grandfather Jacks!"

A slow drumroll much like the beat of the executioner in Magma's fortress. It quickened, the crowd animating with the faster tempo. The drummer sped up into a roll before he finished with three strong beats.

The ring of the final strike in the air, Slate took off, sprinting at the centre of the pitch, the entire field springing to life. The rest of Slate's team took up their positions. The younger team mirrored them. Just one boy ran for the ball while the others spread out.

Although he reached the ball first, Slate charged over the top of it, leading with his right fist. He caught the opposition's runner on the chin, knocking him onto his back.

While another one of Slate's team retrieved the ball, Slate kicked the boy in the head. The boy turned limp. Several teenagers darted onto the pitch and dragged the flaccid kid away by his ankles.

"What the hell?" Matilda said.

Dianna had rejoined them after placing the ball. "I told you there's no holds barred."

A drumroll and cheer took William's attention from the fallen boy. Slate's team ran back into their half while celebrating their first goal.

THE GAME ENDED SEVEN NIL. DESPITE WINNING AS OFTEN AS HE had, Slate still cock-walked around the pitch. Bad losers were hard to tolerate, but bad winners made William's skin crawl.

A wide grin on his smug face, Slate snorted a laugh before bowing to the crowd. "And that, ladies and gents, is how you play tri-rings."

William shouted, "Looked to me like that was a group of stronger boys beating up a group of weaker boys."

"The world's not as black and white as that, kid." Slate winked. "Anyway, do you think you might be able to do better?"

"Maybe."

"Want a game later?"

William waited for one of Cyrus, Max, Artan, or Samson to say no. None of them did. "Sure," he said.

"Don't worry." Slate winked again, this time at Matilda. "We'll go easy on them. Dianna, can you show them to our guest hut, please?"

Dianna nodded. "Sure."

The desire to continue the argument kept William rooted to the spot before Olga tutted at him. "And you told me to keep a lid on it. Hypocritical much?"

AFTER DIANNA LEFT THEM, THEY ALL SAT DOWN IN A CIRCLE IN the small hut and William said, "So, what do you reckon?"

"Slate's a prick," Max said. He'd sat next to Samson, Olga on the other side of the large and now bald man. Had he done that on purpose so he didn't have to be close to her?

William smiled. "But what do you think about staying here?"

"If they shave my head again," Samson said, "I will cut a man's throat."

"This whole gender-separation thing is bullshit," Matilda said. "It's fine for now, but I'm not sure I can stay in a community like this."

"And Slate's a weapon's grade prick," William said. "But you can see how they get away with it."

Both Olga and Matilda replied in unison, "You can?!"

"In Edin, everyone turned eighteen and were then sent outside the walls. I know if I had a kid and it was a girl, I'd be grateful she wouldn't have to sacrifice herself."

"Just her self-worth," Olga said.

"At least she'd be alive."

Before Olga sniped back, Matilda said, "I get what you're saying, and maybe if I'd been raised in a society like this, I'd be okay with it. But I haven't, so while I respect every community's right to act how they see fit, it's not all right by me. At all. But maybe we should give it a week or so and see what this place is really like."

"I won't be oppressed," Olga said.

"I think that's patently obvious," William said. The hard ground had turned his bottom numb, so he pulled himself onto one of the seven beds around the edge of the room. "I stand by you both. Matilda's right; let's give it a week. Maybe we need to see what possibility there is for change. It might surprise us."

Samson scratched his scalp, his lips tight. The smile synonymous with the man had fallen with his hair. Maybe his wild curls hid it before, but his bald head accentuated the thick bags beneath his eyes. He sighed. "I was the only one out of the one hundred from the arena who survived leaving Edin. I went to relieve myself in the night, and when I came back, I found the diseased in our camp. The door I'd left through remained locked. They'd clearly found another way in." He clasped his shaking hands in front of himself. His voice cracked. "They took them down in their sleep. I hope most of them didn't wake up." Tears glazed his eyes, swelling until they ran down his cheeks. "We had kids with us."

William squirmed in the spotlight of Samson's grief and said, "I'm sorry you had to go through that, Samson, I really am. But I'm not sure I see the connection. What do you want to do?"

"I want to rest, William. I'm tired."

Artan and Max nodded their agreement while Cyrus said, "Anything's better than Magma's fortress."

THEY REMAINED IN THEIR HUT FOR SEVERAL HOURS BEFORE Dianna summoned them at Slate's behest. Olga led them out, and although Max followed her, he halted to let William go first, again putting distance between himself and the girl.

William's eyes burned from the change between the gloomy hut and the bright sun. Slate and his tri-rings team had gathered around the pitch's centre circle. The crowd, as numerous as they had been for the game earlier, were muted with anticipation.

"Are you staying?" Slate said.

Olga shrugged. "We'd like to stay here for a week and see if this is the right place for us and we're the right people for this place."

The hairs stood up on the back of William's neck when the already quiet crowd fell silent. Had anyone else responded to Umbriel's generosity with such terms?

Slate nodded. "Ooooo-kay."

Several people in the crowd gasped.

"And you want a game of tri-rings?"

"Matilda and I do. Our team is me, Matilda, William, Max, and Cyrus. Unless you're worried about being shown up by women?"

Silence swept through the place again, some of the retired hunters guffawing and shaking their heads.

"I'll tell you what," Slate said. "We will win, but if you can score at least one point against us, we'll let women play tri-rings after this game. Deal?" He held his hand out towards Olga.

If she considered the offer, it didn't show. Olga clamped hands with Slate, the skin on his hand reddening from how tightly she gripped. "Deal."

While nodding, Slate took in his community. "And so it is, a game not only to welcome our new friends for however long they decide to stay, but also to determine whether we let women play tri-rings from this moment on." He turned back to Olga. "Good luck."

Olga shook her head. "We won't need it."

CHAPTER 26

C loser to the drums than he'd previously been, William flinched with every beat. They currently stood in their own defence zone at one end of the pitch. About two hundred people around them; most, if not all, of Umbriel's community watched on. The retired hunters were in their prime spot directly beside the pitch. Hard to discern from their expressions whether they watched on with concern or judgement. Probably best not to know.

The drumroll reached its crescendo as the people in the community whooped and hollered. They jumped and danced before the final three loud beats. Each one of them sent a kick through William's heart as he took in their opponents.

The final beat still ringing in the drum, Slate sprinted towards the knot, Max meeting him in the centre circle. Slate knocked him to the ground. The strong boy with the scars around his neck followed through, picked up the ball, and charged.

Cyrus dived for the boy and missed, dust kicking up as he landed face down. Before Olga reached the ball carrier, the boy passed it to someone else on his team. Matilda bore down on him, but he offloaded to the person next to him. Slimmer than the others, the boy moved like an eel through water and charged at William.

A moment of weightlessness from where the hunter hit him at full speed, William landed on his back on the dusty ground and the drumroll celebrated Slate's team's first point.

Back in their defensive area, William snapped his head from side to side to combat the pain in his neck. As the drumroll sounded, he fixed on Slate. The boy smiled and then winked at Matilda.

The boy with the scars around his neck had thighs as thick as William's waist. On the final drumbeat, he charged for the ball. Reaching it first, he passed to Slate, who ran straight at Matilda. William and his team had formed a line across the pitch, but William broke it, charging at Slate to protect his love. He dived at the boy, who shimmied and avoided him.

William's move had left a huge hole, the boys passing the ball down the line and exploiting it with another goal.

Matilda's glare told William everything she wouldn't say under the watchful eyes of around two hundred spectators. Hold your position! And if he didn't, he needed to fear her more than the opposition.

They did better on the next play, William letting Matilda fight her own battles. The hunters had avoided contact with the girls until now, but one of them charged Matilda. She met him with force, slamming into him, the crowd cheering when she knocked him on his arse. But he still offloaded the ball, their passing sending William's head spinning as he slammed into the fast boy who'd scored against him initially. The fast boy had already passed. The crowd laughed when they scored again.

"Come on!" Olga screamed, stamping her foot against the dusty ground. Her face red, she shrieked, "That's three nil. We can't go down to these losers!"

The easiest point yet, the hunters moved through them like smoke and went four nil up.

William panted and the dust from the pitch coated his sweat-drenched skin. His entire body throbbed from how many times he'd slammed into the ground. He'd both held his line and broken it. The results were the same. He'd focused on the ball until now. Maybe he needed a different approach. What else did he have to lose?

At the end of the next drumbeat, Olga shrieking like a banshee, William charged Slate. If nothing else, he needed to show the prick he wouldn't be pushed around. Sweat stinging his eyes, his legs on fire with lactic acid, his arms pumping, he ran straight into Slate's palm. The lead hunter hit him so hard it threw his head back first. His legs swung underneath him before he landed on his back, the hard ground driving the wind from his lungs. He had an upside-down view of Slate punching Cyrus and knocking him out cold.

The drumroll signalled five nil, and two teenage boys dragged Cyrus off by his ankles.

"Great!" Olga said. "We're five nil down and there's only four of us left. Can we make a sub?"

Slate laughed and shook his head. "Not in this game, sweetheart."

Her teeth clenched, Olga spoke to her teammates in a low growl. "We can't let these clowns run away with this. We've got to do something. We need to work doubly hard now we're without Cyrus." The boy lay on the sideline, conscious again, but clearly in no state to rejoin the game.

As Slate walked back from going six nil up, he blew Olga a kiss, and the boy with the scars around his neck slapped her arse.

Max's face turned red.

One point for them to win it. Cyrus had gotten to his feet on the sideline. Before he could return to the pitch, one of the older hunters pulled him back and shook his head. He called to William, "It's too dangerous to let him get knocked out again."

Slate reached the ball first. Again. This time he gathered it up, but he stopped, throwing the small rope sphere into the air and catching it, grinning at Olga. "Will you accept women are weaker than men now? You need to learn your place, princess."

The crowd screamed as one. "Man on!"

Before Slate could react, Matilda slammed her forearm into his nose. Even William winced from the crunch of cartilage being crushed.

Slate went down and the ball went up. Matilda caught it before it hit the ground. She paused for a second, giving William, Olga, and Max a chance to get in front of her and form a shield.

Three against four, Max spread his arms wide as he dived forward, taking two of them down with him.

Olga met the one with the scars with a right hook. It stunned him, giving William and Matilda an opening.

One left, the fast one, William tackled him around the waist, dust burning his eyes when they slammed down together. He climbed on top of the boy and got two licks in before the boy fought back. Older, stronger, and more experienced, he caught William on the chin, knocking him backwards as Slate thundered past on Matilda's tail.

Just before the hunters' defence zone, Matilda threw the ball. Slate jumped at her a second too late.

Although Matilda went down under Slate's attack, the drumroll signalled a goal. And not only a goal. The drummer stopped drumming and called, "Two points!"

Matilda's nose bled, the bottom half of her face crimson as she danced in the court to the drummers' beat. All of the women in the crowd cheered and most of the boys. The stony-faced retired hunters watched on, some of them shaking their heads at the mockery of their fine game.

Three loud drumbeats at the end of the roll, and Slate's team tore through them again, scoring their seventh and final point. The crowd celebrated William's team like they'd won the match, charging onto the court and lifting the five of them in the air. They gave them three cheers, led by Rita and Mary, Dianna also close by. They danced and sang, many of them rolling their tongues.

The jubilation died down after about five minutes when Slate grabbed a vacated chair from where the retired hunters had sat, and stood on it.

The spread of two black eyes, his face a swollen mess from where Matilda had taken him down, he smiled, and it looked like he genuinely meant it. "What can I say? If nothing else, I'm a man of my word. From this moment on, women are allowed to play tri-rings. Well done, you've done better than anyone else has in years." He smiled at Olga and Matilda. "You've earned it. Now if you'll forgive me, I need to get cleaned up. I'm not sure I've been hit like that before. But before I head off, we'd like to invite you to a party tonight to celebrate our new guests and how you've made a positive impact on the community already. Will we see you tonight in the main hall?"

William's friends looked at him. If they were to get a proper understanding of this community, they needed to take part. He nodded. "Sure. It seems like something worth celebrating."

CHAPTER 27

"I wonder why they wanted us to come here after dark?" Matilda said as they crossed the tri-rings pitch towards the main hut at the heart of Umbriel's complex.

The dust kicked up around their feet, the smaller particles swirling in the wind, lit by the moon. The tri-rings Matilda had scored in on their left, William smiled. "I know I've already said it, but what a shot!"

"Are you even listening to what I'm saying?" Matilda pointed at the hut. "Why go in there when it's so dark? Surely the party's better outside in the moonlight?"

An inky blackness filled the hut. William squinted as if it would help him see better. "You think they're setting us up for something?"

Olga, Max, and Samson walked just a few paces behind them, Samson's expression as stony now as it had been when they shaved him. Artan and Cyrus were even farther back. The two boys chatted to one another, something Artan hadn't done since they'd freed him from the political district.

Olga said, "Matilda's right to be cautious. We'd be fools to trust them so early on. I know Slate accepted we scored against them in the game, but he has an ego as large as that barn. I can't imagine he's let it go so easily."

"Although," Max said, "they've had plenty of time to do something to us already. We've been seriously outnumbered since we got here. Sure, we should keep our guard raised, but they've gone to a lot of effort if they wanted to screw us over. Why not just kill us when they caught us at the beginning?"

"I wasn't suggesting they were going to kill us," Matilda said. "I just feel uneasy is all."

They were just a few feet from the barn's entrance, the inside still a mystery. The night snapped a chill through William, and the skin at the back of his neck tightened. In a voice only his friends could hear, he said, "We're here now. Let's just be on our guard and make sure we have each other's backs."

The blanket of darkness inside the barn took form. A crowd of silhouettes had been waiting for them. William's legs threatened to betray him, urging him to halt lest they throw him to the ground. Then one of the silhouettes stepped out to meet them. Taller than the rest, broad-shouldered, his hair shaved to stubble.

William nodded at the hunter, who remained naked from the waist up. When he'd gone out hunting, his war paint had been animal's blood, dried brown against his skin. Now he had lines of blue, yellow, and green in a swirling pattern centred around his navel. "Slate, how are you?" William's voice warbled. "Bit dark in there, isn't it?"

Slate paused in the doorway and spread his arms wide, as he liked to do. The entertainer, the showman, the young pup who would one day be top dog. Probably sooner than the retired hunters might like. "Welcome to our main hall. Tonight we wanted to celebrate our new guests and someone scoring points against us in tri-rings." If the lead hunter resented them for it, he hid it well. His broad smile was as white as the moon, his eyes alive.

William and Matilda entered the hut first, Slate stepping aside for them. Their friends followed a second later. As much as William wanted to check they were okay, he kept his eyes ahead and his chin raised.

They reached the middle of the hut, and the silhouettes closed in, encircling them.

Matilda squeezed William's hand so tightly it hurt. If they needed to fight, they would. There might have only been seven of them, but they'd battle like there were twenty. They wouldn't go down easily. William balled his spare fist.

The first drumbeat went off like a thunderclap.

William jumped at the sound.

Then silence.

"Before we start," Slate said, "we want to give praise to Grandfather Jacks. The provider. The high father."

The response came in unison. One hundred voices at least, a shock wave of sound slamming into them from all sides. "Grandfather Jacks."

The silence so complete, William heard the caw of a bird outside. The stillness rendered him mute. Who the hell was Grandfather Jacks?

"You inspire us," Slate said.

The crowd copied him. "You inspire us."

"You guide us."

"You guide us," the crowd responded.

"You teach us."

"You teach us."

Slate's voice circled the group as he walked around them like a shark toying with its prey. The drumbeat again. Then again. It came from a corner of the hut, the steady pulse gaining velocity. "Grandfather Jacks, you light up our world."

The hut then turned from night to day and William screamed, his eyes stinging with the sudden change. He dropped Matilda's hand and shielded his vision against the burn. No matter how many times he blinked, he couldn't see. More drums joined the one from the corner. They hammered the same steady pulse, which gained momentum, galloping towards a drumroll.

William's head spun and he called over the chaos, "Tilly? Where are you?"

Shouts and screams, tongue rolling shrills of celebration, William grew dizzy. His sight slowly returned. The drumrolls slowed and morphed into a strong rhythm, a thudding pulse. The groove inspired the community to dance.

It still hurt his eyes, but William looked at the light source above. A large square covered with glass, it shone as bright as the sun. He only realised he'd had his mouth open when Slate leaned in towards him, dancing to the beat and grinning. The light cast deep shadows across his face, a grotesque mask, his eyes blackened from where Matilda had slammed into him on the tri-rings pitch. "Grandfather Jacks provides."

"Who's Grandfather Jacks?"

"All in good time. Tonight, we party!"

Of all William's friends, Samson seemed the most at ease. Solemn, but at ease. "Do you know what's happening?" William said.

The large and once jovial man shook his head. "It looks like some kind of magic to me."

Although, did it? If any of the others had said that, all of them gawking at the source of light attached to the ceiling, he would have accepted the assessment. Even Artan, who rarely reacted to anything, remained loose jawed as he stood still. But Samson didn't wear the shock of someone in the presence of magic. Nor did he wear the shock of someone caught unawares.

Before William could question him, Samson nodded in Cyrus' direction. The boy had been dragged away from the group by the two older women, Rita and Mary. "You want to watch that one."

"Why do you say that?" William said as Dianna joined them, her hips swaying.

"He seems awfully friendly with the people here. Like he knows them."

"He's a friendly guy."

Samson paused for long enough for William's words to echo through his own mind. For him to take in Cyrus' now wide grin while he danced with the two older women.

Samson shrugged. "Maybe I've gotten him wrong. Look, I don't fancy this tonight. I'm going back to our hut."

The big man cut a path through the dance floor, knocking people aside on his way out of there. A Samson with hair would have smiled and danced like the rest of them. And did he have a point about Cyrus?

Slate and his hunters then closed in, dancing and hollering as they moved towards Olga and Matilda. The hunter with the thick thighs, deep scars, and dark glare grabbed Olga's hands and danced with her. If Max had been anywhere nearby, the hunter might have thought twice. Maybe Max's apparent rejection inspired Olga to get involved, letting the hunter spin her around before he grabbed her hips with both his large hands. William's entire frame tensed when Slate went for Matilda.

The urge to grab the lead hunter coursed through William. To drag him away from the girl he loved, but they were only dancing.

His head spinning from the noise, the light, the writhing bodies, William saw Max move too late to stop him. He shoved the hunter dancing with Olga. The large hunter sent several people flying before he fell, shaking the ground as he landed on his arse.

The drums stopped. The dancing halted. The hunter with the scars remained sitting on the ground, his face red, his hard glare fixed on Max. Before he got to his feet, Slate stepped between them. He raised a halting hand at his friend, which seemed to be enough to calm him. "What's going on, Max?"

As puce as the hunter he'd shoved, Max looked from William to Olga to Slate before he turned around and followed Samson's path out of there, leaving a deeper silence in his wake.

"It's been a long few days for us," William said. "Thank you for the party." He turned on the spot to address the entire hut. "Thank you, everyone, but I think it's a bit soon. The noise, the number of people. We've had a hard time. We've seen thousands die over these past few days, so we're all a bit tightly wound. I think we all need to rest."

"I don't need to rest," Olga said.

"Yes, you do."

Olga clenched her jaw, and although she looked like she might respond, Matilda backed William up as she walked over to Slate. "Thank you," she said. "Thank you so much. Maybe we can get some rest and start again tomorrow?"

The hunter with the scars stood up and Olga said, "I'm so sorry." He nodded.

William and Matilda led the way. Artan, Olga, and Cyrus followed them out of there.

By the time they'd reached the hut, the drums had started again, the shrill calls and whoops of those partying starting anew.

Olga overtook William and Matilda and burst into the hut first. "What the hell was that, Max?"

Max stared at the ground.

"What? You're not going to say anything now? After making a scene like that, you're not going to give me an explanation? If you like me, tell me, because the way you've been since we got you out of that cage makes me think you want *nothing* to do with me." Tears stood in her eyes and she held her hand in his direction. "You know I like you. I'm here if you want me."

Max continued to stare at the ground, the seconds of silence stretching into what felt like hours.

"*Do* you want me?" Olga then tutted, shook her head, and walked over to the edge of their hut, sitting down on one of the beds.

Max kept his head bowed.

"I think we're all tired," William said. "How about we rest up for the night? Tomorrow's a new day; we can start again then." From the look on everyone's faces, none of them believed it would be that simple. Hell, he didn't believe it, but they had to find some way to move on. And they all needed the rest.

CHAPTER 28

It had been the best night's sleep William had had since Edin fell. Light streaked through the gaps in the hut's walls. After stretching, he sat up in bed. Everyone else was already awake.

Matilda had slept in the bed next to him. Her hair disheveled, she scratched her head and smiled. "Morning."

"Hey." His voice was croaky. "How did you sleep?"

"Clearly not as good as you." She shrugged. "But fine. I feel rested."

Deep bags sat beneath Olga's eyes.

"Have you had *any* sleep?" William said.

She raised her eyebrows and looked at Max, who'd slept on the opposite side of the hut from her. He focused on his lap.

Artan and Cyrus talked to one another in hushed tones while Samson lay on his back staring at the ceiling, his hands behind his bald head.

After he'd checked his back pocket for the map, feeling the crunch of the folded paper, William coughed to clear his lungs. "It looks like a nice morning."

"Does it?" Samson said. "I've had enough of this place already."

"It's not so bad," Cyrus said.

"For you. But you know how to suck up to people, don't you?"

"What's that supposed to mean?"

"Also, you and Artan seem to be getting really friendly, whispering to one another like little schoolchildren. It's messing with the mood."

Matilda shook her head. "If anyone's killing the mood, it's you. You're the oldest of all of us by far, yet you're behaving like a petulant teenager. Cyrus and Artan haven't done anything wrong."

"Besides," Olga said, "Max is the one who's made everything awkward."

Max looked up. "So you're going to blame me?"

"Your actions last night were hardly appropriate. I would have danced with you had you not been avoiding me."

"Avoiding—?"

"That's enough," William said. The clangs of pots outside showed the residents of Umbriel were clearly awake or waking up. "They don't need to listen to us arguing."

Olga spoke again. "You think we can show our faces out there after last night? After how *he* behaved."

Matilda said, "What else are we going to do? Wait in here forever? We have to go out there at some point."

"Maybe we need to thank our hosts and move on?" Samson said.

Before anyone else could comment, William said, "Okay, so how about we have a vote? Who wants to stay here, and who wants to move on?" While fixing on Max, he said, "Whatever happens, we will have to go outside and face them."

"I vote we stay for a few days," Olga said. "It's safe and we have beds. I can tolerate their patriarchal bullshit for a short time."

"I'm with Olga," William said. "I feel more rested than I have in ages. It sure beats sleeping in old run-down buildings. Cyrus?"

"I agree with Olga."

Max nodded. "I'm okay with staying. If they don't gut me first."

"I need more rest," Matilda said. "Artan?"

"What does it matter what I think? We're staying."

"Come on then." William got to his feet and reached down to help Matilda stand. "You ready, Max? We might as well go outside and face them now. No point in prolonging it."

The rest of them got to their feet, save Samson, so William walked over and held a hand down to him. "Come on, man, chin up. I know this place isn't perfect, and I know you're still pissed about your hair—"

"You *think?!*"

"But it's the best we've had since Edin fell. Let's give it a few days at least."

Samson had the thick frame of a man. An adult who'd left his childhood behind long ago. He sat up, his wide shoulders tense. A second later, he relaxed them and nodded at William.

They were all on their feet in the gloomy hut, but none of them moved, so William led the way.

The fire was close enough for the smell of cooking meat to hit William the second he emerged. His mouth watered as he waited for his friends.

"Look at the state of that," Olga said, her voice quiet. "Those lazy men are sitting on their arses while the women cook for them. Some of them must be twenty years younger than the women. Why do they get to retire so early?"

"And look at how fat they've grown," Matilda said. "I bet

those older men sit there doing nothing all day. They'd struggle to waddle away from here should their lives depend on it. How do they get so complacent in such a hostile environment?"

"Edin's politicians managed it," William said.

Artan's eyes narrowed. "And look what happened to them."

Olga tutted and raised her voice. "I think it's some kind of bullshit."

"Come on, Olga," William said. "You've managed to get women on the tri-rings team already."

"So you want us to stop there? Be good little girls from now on and learn our place?"

"No."

"Accept the one concession with grace and count our blessings?"

"Just don't try to change everything in the first day. Especially if we're only staying here for a week, and especially after the scene last night."

"You're blaming that on me?"

"I didn't say that."

A ring of hunters had gathered beside the fire. Unlike the retired men, they sat on the ground rather than in padded chairs. Slate's two black eyes had already turned yellow with bruising. He and his hunting party watched William and the others approach. The boy with the scars around his neck wasn't with them.

When they got close, Slate said, "Morning. I hope you slept well."

William lost his words for a few seconds. "Uh … morning."

Rita and Mary approached with a tray of cups filled with water. They handed them out, Rita saying, "It's a little on the warm side, but it's clean."

Matilda knocked hers back in one. "Thank you."

"Now sit," Mary said. "We'll bring you some meat and bread."

The warmth of the fire combated the bite of the bright spring morning. A clear line of sight into the barn, William pointed at the glass sun hanging from the ceiling. "How did you light up the barn last night?"

Although he addressed his question at Mary and Rita, Slate called across to them, "Grandfather Jacks provides." The hunting party around him bowed their heads out of respect.

Too many people watched them, so William nodded and smiled.

No matter how many times it had already happened, when the thud of another drum snapped through the community, William jumped where he sat. The hunters all turned towards the sound. They were clearly expecting this.

Glances passed between William and his friends, but before any of them could speak, the hunter with the scarred neck walked around the side of the hut. Like all the other hunters, he only wore trousers. While the others had painted their bodies with stripes and spirals, every part of his exposed torso and face glistened with fresh animal blood.

"Looks like they're not letting it slide, then," Max said.

Slow and deliberate steps, the hunter fixed on Max as he moved to the steady drumbeat.

William sipped his water to combat his drying throat.

The scarred hunter gripped his spear with both hands.

"I'll bite his throat out before he gets anywhere near you," Olga said.

Max spoke from the side of his mouth. "I can fight my own battles."

Other than the drumbeat and the popping and crackling fire, silence settled over Umbriel. The bloody hunter raised his spear. Much closer and he'd be as good as declaring war.

William bristled where he sat. If he started on Max, he'd be starting on them all.

But the drumbeats stopped. The hunter dropped down onto bended knee and laid his spear on the ground as an offering to Max.

Rita then handed a small container filled with water to the hunter. It had a rag in it.

"I'm sorry I've offended you, Max. If you'll allow me, I'd like to wash your feet."

Although Max opened his mouth to reply, Mary whispered, "Pushing him over wasn't the problem. Refuse him now and you won't walk away from this."

Under the watchful eyes of the entire community, Max stood up.

Two younger boys appeared with a chair like the one the retired hunters sat in. They set it behind Max, who lowered himself into it. When he tried to remove his boots, the hunter knocked his hands away and did it himself, freeing Max's feet before washing them. He avoided eye contact, focusing on the task at hand.

From the other side of the fire, Slate said, "We apologise for offending you and yours. In Umbriel, we dance. We dance with friends and we dance with family. When we danced with your women—"

"She's not my woman," Max said.

Olga's lips tightened.

After a moment's silence, Slate continued, "We're sorry. Please know that. We overstepped the mark and didn't explain our ways. Hawk has offered you his spear. It's yours to do with as you see fit. If you so wish, you may snap it and retire him here. A wild hunter is a hinderance to everyone. Or you can give it to William. He knows how to use one."

William's cheeks burned. Why had he said he could use a spear?

"Please, decide Hawk's fate," Slate said.

"It's been a long few days for us," Max said. "We've all lost loved ones and seen thousands fall to the disease. I was over-emotional last night and take full responsibility for my actions. Hawk did nothing wrong and I apologise."

All the while, Hawk continued to wash Max's feet.

"I wouldn't dream of taking what is clearly a calling away from this man. Please, I'd like it if we started again."

"No need to start again," Slate said. "We've grown together and become better together." He raised his cup of water. "Here's to getting to know one another. Here's to Grandfather Jacks."

The community repeated, "Grandfather Jacks."

Slate said, "Now we eat."

Many of those in the community cheered and the drummers —as often seemed the case in Umbriel—set the mood with a hammering rhythm. Thank the heavens William hadn't reacted to Hawk's approach. They'd made the right choice coming here. He reached out for Matilda and held her hand. "Things are going to get better."

She smiled. "I think so too."

CHAPTER 29

W ould there ever come a time when William could ascend scaffolding and not feel the chasm beside him? The space where his dad should be, chamber pot in hand as they climbed, wondering if they'd see another eviction. The evictions had been fun to witness as a child, but as he'd grown older, he revelled much less in the punishment of others. He had less faith in Edin's propaganda that those receiving the punishment were the bad guys. He knew Mr. P; he knew the truth.

Umbriel's scaffolding shook with the sheer weight of people climbing it. Like many things, they used today's event as a cause for celebration, drumming and dancing, singing and shouting. Many people wore drums, but they also had one built into the top of the wall. About six feet tall, it had a diameter of at least four feet and it barked the deepest beat.

The large structure creaked and swayed. Every movement sent a lurch through William's stomach. But surely they'd partied like this on here in the past? He had to shout to be heard over the celebrations. "Has the scaffolding ever collapsed?"

Slate walked just ahead of him, half naked from the waist up, a spear in his hand. The lead hunter laughed and shook his head. "No, we've never had a problem. I mean"—he looked up at the next level, the entire structure groaning as it swayed —"it could happen, but what's the point in worrying about it?"

Well, that helped. Matilda walked behind William, Artan behind her; Cyrus, Max, Samson, and then Olga at the back. Many of Edin's residents had already climbed the scaffolding, jostling for position along the top walkway amongst mostly women and children. Maybe the retired hunters stayed on the ground for this one.

Like with the scaffolding in Edin, the structure had ramps leading from one level to the next. William followed the hunters to the top, gasping when he looked over the side at the sea of diseased. The first time he'd looked at one since entering Umbriel, the slight respite had made him almost forget the horror. Crimson stares, snapping jaws, palsied movements. An insatiable desire for destruction.

"That large drum," Slate said, "is designed to call the creatures to us."

"Why?"

"So we can see if there are any young hunters ready to join us outside the walls."

The gaggle of teenage boys at the other end of the top floor suddenly made some sense. They were afforded more space than the spectators and they gathered near a bucket filled with spears.

Now they'd climbed to the top platform, Slate nodded at the wannabe hunters. "You need to join that line and go through the trials too. I'm sure it'll be a breeze for you, but let them go first, yeah? We don't want to disparage them before they've given it a try."

William stood aside to let Artan, Cyrus, Max, and Samson through before he joined the end of the line.

As Matilda and Olga followed him, Slate blocked their way with his arm. "Not you two."

"What?" Olga said. "This again?"

William moved close to his small firecracker friend. He spoke for the benefit of her and Matilda. "While I agree with you and would feel much safer in a hunting pack if you were both in it, we can't try to change too much too soon. Let's not have this conversation now, yeah?"

"What? You want me to know my place, is that it?"

"You don't need to fight me about this. Believe me, if I could give you my spot, I would."

"Why did you tell them you could throw a spear?" Matilda said.

William shrugged. "Ego. How could I not feel inferior around that lot?" The hunters lined up, ready to watch the trials. "But we need to be sensible and pick our battles. I'm not suggesting we don't fight them, but please, for the sake of everyone else in the group, let it slide for now."

"It's some kind of bullshit, if you ask me." Olga folded her arms across her chest.

"I agree. But maybe me making a tit of myself will help you take your mind off it."

It took a gentle tug from Matilda to coax Olga away. They moved over to one side to be with the drummers and spectators. Hawk, the hunter with scars around his neck, sidled close to Olga.

Slate might not have been able to hear their conversation, but he clearly witnessed the outcome. He thanked William with a nod before raising a hand to silence the drummers. Squalls and screams from the diseased horde, the lead hunter shouted over them. "Praise be to Grandfather Jacks, the high father."

The community responded in unison, "The high father."

"Now I know you're all aware of the rules for joining the

hunt, but our guests aren't, so I will explain it for their benefit. Every few days, we open trials to see if any of the young hunters are ready to join us. They need to call out the diseased they're going to hit and take them down with a spear. If they do this three times in a row, they're ready to hunt."

The crowd were agitated, many of them bouncing or swaying. Many were smiling.

"So there's little else to say other than, *let the trials begin!*"

The crowd cheered, the drums banging while the first of the boys pulled a spear from the bucket and walked to the edge. He used his weapon to point down into the crowd of diseased. His voice rang out from the wall, a warrior's cry. "The bald one with the blue coat." He pulled his spear back and launched it.

The crowd gasped as if frustrated for the boy when he missed by several feet. They clapped him as he walked away.

Several more wannabes launched their spears over the wall's spiked top. All of them missed on their first attempt.

The next boy was either several years older than the others, or he'd developed early. As tall as William at over six feet, he had a thick upper body and a square jaw. The morning sun glistened off his dark skin. "The one with a missing eye."

He loosed the spear, the projectile travelling so fast William lost sight of it. Until it embedded in the creature he'd nominated, blinding it by slamming into its other eye. The crowd erupted, dancing and singing as the boy retrieved his second spear.

"The fat one with the afro."

Two out of two, when the boy returned with his third spear, William's entire body tensed. How could he follow him?

"The woman with the blonde hair." He loosed his spear with the same pace and power as his previous two throws.

The scaffolding rocked and swayed when the woman went down. The hunters rushed to the boy and clapped his back.

They led him to a pot filled with deer blood, decorating him with similar patterns to their own. Although, the effect was diminished because of his skin's pigmentation.

Olga and Matilda stood out in the smiling crowd, both of them stony faced as they watched on. Olga might have been the more vocal of the two, but William knew Matilda's hard frown. Her fury would spill over at some point.

When all the young hunters had taken their turns and failed to meet the requirements to go beyond the walls, Cyrus stepped up.

The same silence as he moved to the edge, spear in hand. He pointed the tip of his weapon down, his voice warbling as he said, "The woman with the black hair and burn scars." He grunted with the effort of the throw, and his spear stuck the fat belly of a man at least ten feet away.

The silence held until Artan stepped up, Cyrus clapping him on the back as he walked away. Sallow cheeks, dark bags beneath his eyes, the skinny boy said, "The man with the long hair next to the woman in white."

Artan nailed him, the crowd erupting once more.

His next spear ready, he pointed it down again. "The woman in white." He hit his second target.

Just before nominating the final diseased, Artan glanced at his sister. She'd turned ashen and bit her bottom lip. "The woman with the red top."

Artan missed by such a distance, William winced in antici-pation of the crowd's boos. He'd clearly failed on purpose.

"So close," Slate said as Artan passed him. "Maybe next time."

When Max hit one, Hawk clapped louder and longer than anyone else, winking at him as he stepped up for his second attempt. Max's cheeks flushed red and he missed by several feet.

Samson missed on his first attempt.

By the time William picked up a spear, his hands were slick with sweat. The crowd had fallen silent, making Slate much easier to hear. "I'm excited for this one. I believe William is something of an expert hunter. Come on, William, show them what you can do."

William's throat locked and his words wouldn't come. He saw every face both below and around him, fixed on him with expectation. He coughed, half-heaved, and coughed again, banging his chest with a closed fist as if that would help him get his words out. "That one."

Slate laughed. "Uh, which one, William?"

"The old man with the long white beard." He yelled as he launched his spear. His shot made Cyrus' look accurate. Fifteen feet wide, maybe even more, the silence closed in on him, suffocating him.

Slate's jaw fell and it took him several seconds before he clapped his hands. "Let's hear it for our challengers. Well done, all of you."

As William passed the head hunter, the crowd clapping and cheering, Slate leaned close to him. "We'll get you practicing with one of the retired hunters. It's probably just getting used to the feel of our spears."

It would have been easier if he'd been a prick about it. William kept his attention on the walkway as he passed his friends and walked down the ramp to the lower level of the scaffolding. Why had he said he knew how to throw a spear?

CHAPTER 30

Now the hunters had gone out for the day, William, Max, Cyrus, Artan, and Samson returned to the scaffolding on the back wall. They waited on the top level, the wild meadow of the wastelands stretching away from them. Many of the diseased from earlier had now dispersed, the fresh spring breeze free of their vinegar taint.

Slate had told them they'd meet a retired hunter up there, and it didn't take long for an older man to shuffle up the final ramp. A man in his fifties, he had closely cropped white hair and crow's feet streaking away from his green eyes. He walked with a limp and a scowl.

"What's this?" Max said from the side of his mouth. "The man's ancient. What's *he* going to show us?"

"You'd do well to know I have ears like a hawk," the old man said. "I might look washed up, but they've asked me to teach you because you all need it. So instead of being a dickhead, maybe you should keep your mouth shut and see if you might learn something?"

Max's blue eyes narrowed, and he opened his mouth as if to respond, but clearly thought better of it.

Just a foot separating them, the man halted, but he leaned even closer so their noses were nearly touching. "The correct response is *yes, sir.* You'd do well to remember that. I'd hate to throw you over this wall for insolence."

Max ran his tongue across his lips and his nostrils flared.

"Well?" the old man said.

Max nodded and spoke slowly. "Yes, sir."

"Right, I'm here because you lot are useless. You listen to me and I'll teach you something about throwing a spear. I might not be able to run anymore, but I can still take the wings off a fly's back with one throw. They used to call me Bullseye because there's no one better. Although, I'm a lot older now and prefer the name my mother gave me. You can call me Greg, or sir. Anything else and I'll gut you." He stepped close to Samson. "You hear me?"

Larger and fitter than the man addressing him, Samson might have still been stuck in his petulant funk because they shaved his head, but his maturity shone through and he nodded. "Yes, Greg."

"Right!" Greg pulled five spears from the bucket and handed them out. He slammed several beats against the large drum. "Let's see what you chumps have in you. I've been told if I threw you over this wall, you'd struggle to hit the ground. You!" He pointed at Artan.

Artan walked to the edge of the wall and threw his spear mid-step. The projectile punctured the face of a fat woman, burst out the back of her head, and dropped her.

Greg whistled. "Impressive." He reached out and took Cyrus' spear from him and handed it over.

Artan nailed an old man next. A bent back, the hunched man fell forwards and hit the ground face first.

Before Greg could ask for it, William handed over his spear.

The diseased Artan aimed for screamed as the spear glanced off the side of its face, but he didn't kill it.

"Well, I must—"

Before Greg could say anything else, Artan walked away, down the ramp to the next level, and disappeared from sight.

"Fair enough." Greg shrugged and turned to Cyrus. "You next."

Cyrus grunted as he let the spear fly. It wobbled mid-flight and landed sideways on the ground. Samson snorted a laugh and shook his head.

Max next, he hit two like Artan had. And like Artan, he left.

Samson missed, although at least his spear stuck in the ground.

William's turn. When he gripped the spear, Greg said, "Are you trying to throw it or throttle it? Hold it gently. If you can't hold it right, how do you expect to hit anything?" The older man helped William by adjusting his grip for him, his own hands thick and calloused.

The spear flew true. It might have stuck into the ground like a planted flag, missing the diseased he'd aimed for by several feet, but it flew true. William did his best to hide his smile in the face of Greg's disdain.

THE SUN HAD REACHED ITS ZENITH BY THE TIME THEY WERE done for the day several hours later. Samson and Cyrus left one after the other, Cyrus apparently waiting so he didn't have to walk with the large man. William hung back to accompany Greg.

They walked side by side down the first two levels. When they reached the ground, William said, "I'd like to say thank you for your time today."

"Go on, then."

"Go on what?"

"Say thank you."

William smiled. "Thank you. I know it must be frustrating to teach us. I believe the custom here is to wash another person's feet, if you'll let me?"

For the first time that day, Greg's frown lifted ever so slightly. Still a frown, and a hard one at that, but it shifted from open aggression to disdain. "Come with me."

As one of the older members of the community, Greg had his own hut away from the main crowd. The walls were adorned with beautiful paintings of landscapes. For paint, the artist had used dirt, grass, and blood. "Are these yours?" William said.

By way of reply, Greg handed William a pot filled with water. It had a grey cloth swirling in it. He sat down in a padded seat much like the ones used by the retired hunters near the tri-rings pitch.

"Why don't you come to community events?" William asked.

Still, Greg said nothing and removed his boots and socks, his old feet twisted and gnarled, his toenails like horns.

WHEN WILLIAM HAD FINISHED, GREG CHOOSING TO SIT IN silence for the entire time, William stood up and bowed to the retired hunter. The man dipped his head in return before William left. "Thanks again, Greg. See you tomorrow."

CHAPTER 31

As William drew close to the large hut, he peered through the entrance at the glass sun. How had they lit the place at night, and who the hell was Grandfather Jacks? But the questions left him when he got a clear sight of the tri-rings pitch, and specifically Max and Samson teaching the younger kids in the community the art of sword fighting.

Several retired hunters between him and his friends, they shook their heads and tutted.

"What are you doing?" William said, keeping his voice low.

Max shrugged. "We're teaching them how to sword fight."

"But they *hate* sword fighting here. Look around."

The stick Max had used as a makeshift sword fell slightly limp when he met the retired hunters' judgement.

"Sorry," William called up to them. "We were just trying to help entertain the kids."

"By making fools of yourselves?" one of the retired hunters said.

"And them," another one added.

"Come on." William ushered his friends away before either of them said something they'd have to answer for.

On the way to their hut, the main gate's metal chains rattled. Two of the wannabe hunters who'd been at the spear throwing that morning turned a winch on either side to lift the large wooden door.

About twenty hunters entered, blood stripes on their faces and torsos. Everyone in the community stopped what they were doing and applauded their return. While some of them remained stoic, the boy who'd passed the spear throwing test that morning wore a grin so wide it nearly touched his ears. A dead deer slung across the back of his broad shoulders, he raised his spear aloft to even more cheers.

As more of the hunters filed into the place, William sidled closer to Max and Samson. "I'm guessing the hunt went well, then."

"Looks that way," Max said.

MAYBE WILLIAM IMAGINED THE ATMOSPHERE THE NEXT DAY. Samson had sniped at Cyrus most of the previous evening, the boy finally admitting defeat by going to bed early. Were it not for Matilda by his side, he might not have slept a wink. But he couldn't worry about everyone else's problems. They were adults, or as good as; they could look after themselves.

Still ill at ease when they went for breakfast, maybe William also imagined the hostility from those in the community. Maybe he projected the turmoil within his own party on them. Even if they were pissed off, he couldn't blame them. So far, they'd eaten their food and offered nothing in return other than sword fighting lessons.

They all ate in silence. Afterwards, the girls went with Rita and Mary to help in the fields, while the boys returned to the back wall to meet Greg.

A similar routine to the previous morning, except Artan hit three diseased and left, while Max only hit two. Samson hit one this time, and Cyrus would probably do better throwing rocks.

William's turn, he tried to loosen his shoulder and arm while he wound back and took aim. This time, when he threw his spear, not only did it fly true, but it scored a direct hit, the sharp point entering the back of a diseased's head and punching out through the front of its face.

Greg gave them more time and William scored several more headshots. Never two in a row, but he killed more today than he had yesterday. Samson and Cyrus left again, and William returned with Greg to his hut.

"He doesn't say much," Greg said while William cleaned his feet.

"Who?"

"The moody boy you have with you. The one with the gaunt face and brooding stare."

"Artan?"

"That's right. And the other one says too much."

"Max."

"Yes, Max. What's Artan's story?"

"He was in prison."

Greg raised his bushy white eyebrows.

"He was innocent."

"They all are."

"Well, not innocent, but his crime was entirely justified."

"The second we start justifying crime, we lose our civility."

"He killed his dad."

"And that's justified?"

"His dad had killed his mum."

"Quite the family drama."

"The man beat Artan and Matilda for years; they're brother and sister."

"I could tell. And you're sweet on her?"

Heat flooded William's cheeks and he focused on washing Greg's feet. "We have been since we were kids."

Still not a smile, but the more time William spent around Greg, the more the old man's frown lifted.

"Greg, can I ask you something?"

"You just did."

"Did you do all these paintings?"

There must have been fifty or so, one of them taking up an entire wall in the basic hut. "I did."

"They all look like the same place." Sandy beaches, a bright sun in the sky, birds flying overhead, boats floating in the sea. "I've never seen somewhere so beautiful, other than in some of the books from the old world, but I thought they were just stories. Where is it?"

"It's the place I dream about when I sleep. A place I long to live in rather than this hideous wasteland."

William's mouth hung open. He never tired of looking at the wonderful paintings. "I'm going to try to visit it in my dreams too. If you don't mind, that is?"

"You're welcome any time."

WILLIAM BUMPED INTO HIS FRIENDS WHEN HE LEFT GREG'S hut. After training, they'd gone to work in the fields. Max and Olga walked together. The fact they were so close to one another and not arguing seemed like progress. Samson walked alone. Artan, Cyrus, and Matilda talked amongst themselves. After holding hands with Matilda and checking she was okay, William and Max moved away from the group.

"What's going on?" William said. "With you and Olga?"

"I don't know what to do, William. I like her, I really do."

"And she likes you. So what's the problem?"

"It's not fair."

"What's not?"

"I can't be with her. What do you think will happen the second we kiss?"

William gasped and clapped his hand to his mouth. "Oh, shit! I didn't think. At all. Shit."

"Exactly. So what am I supposed to do? Get into a relationship with her but deprive her of intimacy? It would be torture for me, so how can I expect her to tolerate it? She should choose someone else. Hawk seems like a nice guy."

William rolled his eyes. "Maybe you need to let her make that choice rather than push her away?"

Max shrugged. "My head's a mess." He walked off before William could say anything else.

WHEN WILLIAM NAILED THREE DISEASED IN A ROW THE NEXT day, Greg not only smiled, but he shrieked and punched the air. "And there it is! I knew you had it in you!" Even Cyrus had hit two in a row that morning in training. But all the others had already left while William remained back and practiced some more. "I'm going to tell Slate to let you take the trials again tomorrow. They want to take you out hunting soon, and I think you're ready."

"Thank you, Greg."

"My pleasure."

"I'm going to miss our training sessions. With all the other nonsense that's been going on, it's given me something to focus on."

When they reached the ground, Greg said, "Today, I wash your feet."

SAT IN GREG'S COMFY CHAIR WHILE HE HAD HIS FEET CLEANED, William studied the paintings again. "I can almost smell the salt in the sea. At least, what I expect it to smell like."

Greg smiled.

"Greg, who's Grandfather Jacks?"

The older man's smile faltered and he kept his focus on William's feet. "He's the high father. The one we look up to."

"That doesn't answer my question."

"Some questions are better off unanswered."

Before William could ask him anything else, Greg stood up while drying his hands. "Can I offer you some advice, William?"

"You always have before."

Although Greg smiled again, his eyes lost focus. "This place ... it's toxic. You might have safety, but I think all the problems in your group will feel better when you're away from here. This isn't somewhere you should stay. Not if you want all the things you've told me about. Matilda's a special girl, and Olga doesn't deserve it either."

"What are you talking about, Greg?"

"Just move on soon, yeah?" He held his hand out for William to shake. "It's been a pleasure training with you. I won't be at the ceremony tomorrow—I tend to stay away—but good luck. Learning how to hunt like us will stand you in good stead. Take that with you when you go."

Words didn't seem to cut it, so William wrapped Greg in a

hug, the man squeezing so tightly it took William back to being in his dad's arms. His eyes filled with tears and his throat burned. Unable to speak, he left the old man's hut. Tomorrow he'd become a hunter. Who knew what would happen after that?

CHAPTER 32

Having spent the past three days on the scaffolding with his friends while Greg oversaw their training, William had grown used to being on the tall structure this early in the morning. He closed his eyes and filled his lungs, the strong and fresh breeze helping his digestion, his stomach full from a breakfast of deer meat and bread. He'd never eaten so well as he had since he'd come to Umbriel.

Twenty minutes later, William's moment of peace existed as no more than a distant memory. Most of the community had joined them, the entire wooden frame shaking and swaying. Their raucous need for celebration exploded from them as if they delivered it in an open challenge to the heavens. Whatever you throw at us, we will endure. Grandfather Jacks provides.

The drums summoned the diseased from far away, the higher-pitched rhythm from the smaller ones riding on the back of the deep bass drum boom from the top of the wall. A dense pack of foetid creatures gathered like groupies, nudging and shoving one another as they jostled for position. Hundreds of glazed crimson stares, their mouths working as if their jaws ached, spasms snapping through them. The sight turned the back of William's knees weak.

Greg had been true to his word and hadn't shown. The man's absence sent a pang through William's chest. He considered him a friend and would have liked him to witness his improved performance. And what had he meant when he'd told him to move on? When should they move on and why? What didn't they know about Umbriel?

The elders might have disapproved of the sword training and how William and his friends worked in the fields with the women, but Rita, Mary, and Dianna were on the top level of the scaffolding, showing their support, as were most of the community's children. At least they'd won over some of Umbriel's citizens. When they proved what they could now do with their spears, surely they would convince more of them.

The crowd parted for Slate, who appeared on the top floor of the scaffolding with his usual wide grin. Two hunters walked behind him: Hawk, his face twisted like he'd eaten something foul, and the newest hunter to come through the trials, also stoic, but not as openly hostile as his scarred partner.

Slate stopped just a few feet away from William and used his hand to cut through the air, silencing the drummers and crowd. "Bullseye tells me you've come a long way in the past three days. That all of you might be ready to join us on our next hunt."

William shrugged. "We've been trying hard."

"So I've heard. Well, what are we waiting for? Show us what you can do."

Artan had spent the least amount of time training. He'd thrown his spears and left every day, yet he stepped up first, using the end of his spear to point into the crowd. "The tall black man with a gash across his face."

The boy threw his spear with such force, it made a *swoosh!*

It sailed directly into the face of his intended target, dropping the diseased freak.

The crowd gasped.

"The small white boy with the red top." Maybe distasteful to take down an infant, and the silence of the crowd afterwards suggested they felt the same, but if Artan cared about their reaction, it didn't show. Besides, he'd just nailed a smaller target. That had to be worth something, right? The spear had sailed straight through the kid's face, and it pinned him to the ground.

"The white woman with the blonde curly hair." No way would William have aimed for a target so far away. *Swoosh!* Artan took her down too.

Wild celebration shoved the somber atmosphere aside. The crowd cheered and shouted and the drummers played, the galloping boom of it sending rolling thunder away from the scaffolding out across the wastelands.

Again, Slate chopped the air to silence everyone. "Well done, Artan." Several hunters, including Hawk and the newest recruit, approached Artan, helped him free of his top, and painted his face with the blood of their latest kill. They drew lines that accentuated the boy's already angled bone structure, and added extra shade to his sallow cheeks. He looked like he'd been brought back from the dead.

Max next. He too nailed three shots, although he didn't showboat like Artan, making three safe shots one after the other, checking to see if Olga watched him each time.

While the hunters prepared Max, Cyrus hit two. The boy had come a long way in three days, but he still didn't make the grade. Samson missed on his first shot.

William's turn, he pulled a tight-lipped smile at Matilda before approaching the bucket filled with spears. Greg still hadn't arrived. The man hadn't promised him anything, but it still took him back to the day he went on national service. The day he expected his dad to say goodbye to him, but the man couldn't cope and went to work instead.

A warble in his voice when the community fell silent, William pointed down at an older woman. "The woman with the black dress and white hair."

The spear shattered the front of her skull with a *crunch!*

Matilda smiled and waited for William to get close to the bucket of spears before she said, "Well done. You can do this. I believe in you."

"The fat man in the blue top."

Crack. The spear went through his left temple and burst out of his right cheek. The man went down.

His pulse slamming through him, his legs weak, William shivered from his adrenaline rush and wiped his now damp palms on his trousers before retrieving the third spear. "The man with the red face and big blond hair."

When William missed, the crowd gasped. Many groaned their disappointment.

Only a walk of a few feet to get to Slate, but it felt like miles as the silence from the crowd held, the diseased snarling and hissing below.

While wincing as if pained by what he'd seen, Slate looked around to make sure he had the crowd's attention before he said, "Greg's told me how hard all of you have worked, especially you, William. This is unprecedented, but you've all already been outside the walls, so I'd still like to invite you to join us on our hunt today. Cyrus, you were close enough. And Samson, I know you can't throw a spear, but you can carry our prey."

Samson's tanned skin glowed red as he fixed on Slate. He did well to keep whatever thoughts running through his mind to himself.

"The rest of you," Slate said, "should be powerful allies outside these walls."

"What about me and Matilda?" Olga said.

"You've already managed to get women playing tri-rings."

"So?"

"Don't push it, Olga. There are only—"

Instead of letting Slate finish, Olga walked to the bucket of spears and retrieved one. A low-level hum came from where the crowd murmured to one another. What was this girl doing?

"That one there," Olga said, pointing down. "The one about the same build as you, Slate. He has a shaved head like you too." She nailed the tall, shaven-headed diseased.

"Oh, look, there's one with cuts around its neck. Given time, they'd turn into scars." She winked at Hawk before loosing the spear. It slammed through the eye of the second one.

"And finally, that fat old man. He looks like one of the lazy hunters who thinks this world's here to make his life better." She threw the final spear with such force, she grunted as she loosed it.

The crowd gasped as the spear buried into the man's groin. The creature yelled, but it didn't go down.

Olga spun on Slate, one hand on her hip and her eyebrow raised. "Now tell me I'm not good enough."

"That wasn't the point I was trying to make. I think you're too hot-headed. If I had a man who behaved like you, I'd be frightened to take him out hunting with me. You can't rely on a berserker."

William had spent enough time with Olga to read the signals. Her top lip lifted in a snarl, her brow furrowed. Before she could attack Slate, he grabbed her arm. "Don't put us all in danger for this, Olga. We can't change everything now. If you attack him, you're drawing all of us into a fight we don't want."

"Look," Slate said, "taking too many new people hunting is

a serious risk, so how about we take the men today, and you come with us on the next trip?"

"Why don't you swap me for one of them? I'm as good as Max and Artan. I'm better than William and Cyrus."

"The matter's closed, Olga. Please understand the decision's been made. We'll talk again in the future." Before Olga could continue the conversation, Slate turned to the rest of the crowd. "We have our hunting party for today. Thank you everyone for your support. We hope to return with more deer and other meat than ever before."

As the crowd made their way from the scaffolding, Olga and Matilda leading their group down the wooden structure, Artan grabbed William's left arm and pulled him back.

The bags beneath his eyes had been darkened by the lines of dried blood around them. He said, "I'm not sure we're making the correct choice here to go out hunting with them. I don't trust them."

Greg's warning came back to William. "Why do you say that?"

"It's just a feeling. Like with Samson."

"Samson's done nothing but help us."

"So far. Although, I'm not sure Cyrus would agree."

"And we can trust Cyrus?"

"I do."

The slightest shift of Artan's attention over William's right shoulder gave him a heads-up.

The same grin he'd worn for the duration of the trials, Slate approached them. "Look, William, I wanted to apologise. We've not made it easy for you in Umbriel, but we need to test people to see if they're the right fit for this place. We have our ways, which I appreciate can be alien for many." He held his hand out for William to shake, his grip strong. "I just wanted to say it will be an honour to have you out hunting with us. You too, Artan. You look as good as any of us."

A dipped nod of appreciation, Artan maintained eye contact with Slate.

"Anyway," Slate said, "we'll see you by the front gates in about half an hour, yeah?"

"See you soon," William said.

When the lead hunter had walked from earshot, William turned back to Artan. "Look, I get your caution. I don't see us staying here long. If nothing else, Olga won't last too much longer. But I reckon we should spend a few more days to eat and rest before we move on. Besides, learning how to hunt will only work in our favour when we're back out there. What do you say?"

Artan nodded again. It looked like he fought to get the words out. "I trust you, William. You're the boss."

The scaffolding now clear, they walked off it together. "Slate's right, you know," William said.

Artan raised an eyebrow.

"I can't wait to see you using that spear. I reckon you might teach the hunters a thing or two."

Not quite a smile, but the twitching of Artan's lips lifted to about as close as he'd gotten since they busted him out of the justice department building. "I think so too."

CHAPTER 33

William lined up with Max on his left and Artan on his right. Cyrus stood next to Artan and Samson at the opposite end of the line to the boy he hated, and maybe rightly so. Would William find out the truth about the kid from national service too late? Rita and Mary worked on Max and William while Dianna worked on Artan. Two other women from the community tended to Cyrus and Samson.

First they stripped them of their tops, William's torso tightening from the slight chill. The sun shone down on them, as it had done for days, but they were weeks away from summer. In an attempt to prevent himself from shivering, he focused on where the sun's warmth touched his skin and tried to pull it deeper into him.

A quick check of his back pocket, the crunch of the map still there. William flinched while Rita drew lines of blood on his face, running her fingers just below his eyes. The blood dried against his skin. Max and Artan only needed a touch-up because they'd already been decorated on the scaffolding.

Most of the community watched on, Matilda and Olga in

the crowd, Olga with her arms folded across her chest. William said, "Do the retired hunters normally come to this?"

After she'd looked over both shoulders, Rita nodded. "But don't worry about them. They don't like anything new."

The elders wouldn't need to get used to them. One hunt and they'd be out of there. The conversations William had had with Artan and Greg had convinced him. Just one hunt.

Beyond the tri-rings pitch, leaning against the large hut with the glass sun, stood Greg. The retired hunter saluted and William smiled. At least he had one of the older generation on his side.

Once Rita had finished, she grabbed William with her warm hands and pulled him towards her, kissing his forehead. "You look after yourself out there, you hear me?"

"Do you know something you're not telling me?"

"What do you mean?"

Greg had already left, but his warning remained. If Rita knew something, her brown eyes hid it well. "Look after the girls, yeah?"

Rita nodded. "I'll do my best."

All the women finished at the same time, and as they walked away, Artan said, "What was that about?"

"I'm not sure. But I was thinking about what you said; we'll go on one hunt and then leave this place, okay?"

Before Artan responded, the apprentice hunters approached, each of them holding a bucket of spears.

Slate and the others had stood aside, but the lead hunter now stepped forward. "You all need to pick two spears each. One for dealing with the diseased, which will be the spear you carry so you're always ready. And the other one's for hunting. Make sure the heads don't rub against one another. We don't want them getting contaminated with diseased blood."

Although William had spent some time with Greg, there were so many questions he hadn't asked him. Like how do you pick a good spear? Logic told him the straightest were best, so he fished through the barrel of spears and grabbed what he believed to be the straight ones. With so many spectators, he could hardly get them all out and look. An amateur pretending he knew what he was talking about. All the gear and no idea. No, thanks. He'd make do with his choices.

Adopting his usual posture, Slate spread his arms wide and turned his back on the new hunters, facing the women, children, and apprentices gathered there. "May Grandfather Jacks watch over us on this hunt." He looked up, addressing the clouds, "We have several new faces who need to know you in their hearts. Please grant them courage and strength like you give to us every day. To the provider and the high father."

The crowd echoed him. "The provider and high father."

As Slate stepped away, he smiled at William and winked. William dipped a nod in return. Despite all the hostility over the past few days, at least the hunter had backed away from Matilda.

Matilda and Olga approached the boys. Olga's tanned skin still glowed red. She needed to find a release soon. Hopefully, she'd find it in private. Matilda wore a mask of calm. The fury would be burning as hot in her, but she had more self-control. Now wasn't the time.

While chewing on her bottom lip, Olga glanced at one of the buckets of spears. William leaned close to Max. "She's going to kick off again. Have a word with her, yeah?"

"You think *I* can change her mind? Let's just see what she has to say."

Olga and Matilda walked past the spears. Olga approached Max while Matilda went to Artan.

Olga poked Max in the centre of his exposed chest, knocking him back a step. "You'd best come back."

William smiled. Olga even approached flirting like she wanted a fight.

Matilda hugged Artan. "*All* of you best come back!"

When Olga leaned close to Max, William winced. At the last moment, Max turned aside so she kissed his cheek.

Where Olga had been red just a few seconds ago, she now glowed with shame, her brown eyes widening.

Max stepped back from her and held her hands. "Look, Olga, this won't work between us."

Did he really need to say that now?

"I—"

The *crack* of Olga's right hook rang out. The crowd fell silent.

Tears stood in Max's eyes, a welt on his left cheek where she'd hit him. If William had been hit that hard, his eyes would be watering too. Max lifted his chin. "You should be with someone who makes you happy."

Olga shook where she stood, and twitches ran through William's body as he readied himself to step between them. But instead of going for Max again, she walked to the group of hunters gathered by the wall, grabbed Hawk, and kissed him.

The kiss seemed to last a lifetime, Hawk reaching down and holding Olga's bottom. Although Max stared straight ahead, his eyes watered more than before.

"Couldn't you have saved that for a better time?" William said.

"She just tried to kiss me."

Olga stormed back to their hut, while Hawk grinned for the first time since William had met him.

The metal chains jangled behind them from where the apprentices lifted the gate. Matilda stepped closer to William and pressed her palm over his heart. "Just come back alive, okay?"

William nodded before Matilda kissed him and followed the path taken by Olga. He spoke to Artan from the side of his mouth. "Why am I starting to think even one hunting trip might be a bad idea?"

CHAPTER 34

Several days inside Umbriel's walls and eating more than he had in his entire life had left William gasping to keep up with the hunters' frenetic pace. They moved through the long grass as if their feet didn't touch the ground. In contrast, William padded after them as if gravity's pull had trebled.

From the gasps and pants of those around him, his friends were struggling too. Samson especially, his red face glistening with sweat, his mouth stretched wide, desperate for more air.

The newest hunter to the group—the one who'd won the trials several days ago—loosed his spear. William only saw the diseased when it went down to the attack, tripping and rolling several times in the long grass. The spear stuck straight up like a flagpole. The hunter retrieved it without breaking stride.

Several more hunters took down several more diseased. Every time, they speared them and retrieved their weapons without upsetting the group's momentum.

Were William able to breathe, he might have complimented the hunters on their skills. Instead, he had to settle for watching on in awe while his legs burned with fatigue.

Hawk slowed his pace, dropping back from the main group

so Max caught up to him. "Looks like your girl's chosen. I can't blame her. She clearly likes a man with a bit more about him. She knows an alpha when she sees one."

Max stared straight ahead, locked into a deep breathing rhythm.

After Hawk sped up to rejoin the leading pack, Cyrus said, "Why did you turn her away?"

The muscles in Max's face tensed.

"Why don't you mind your own business, Cyrus?" Samson said.

Before it could escalate, the hunters ahead of them stopped.

While William and his friends caught their breath, Slate approached. "Wait here. We want to show you something."

Fighting the urge to either bend over and rest on his knees, or sit down, William linked his fingers behind his head to open his lungs and spun on the spot. They'd stopped in the centre of a ring of trees. Ten to fifteen of them, evenly spaced, they were green and bushy. The hunters split up and climbed them. Within a few seconds, every one of them had vanished from sight.

Now he couldn't see Slate, William struggled to even place the location of his voice, other than to know which tree it came from. Were he to aim a spear at the lead hunter right now, he'd probably miss him by a mile. "This is how we hunt. We climb these trees and wait. Nailing unsuspecting deer is much like nailing the diseased from Umbriel's back wall."

Drumming came from the trees surrounding them. The same beat they played in Umbriel, it called over the wild meadow.

"How do the drums help when catching deer?" Max said, spinning on the spot.

William called in the direction of Slate's tree. "What are you doing?"

The beats accelerated and grew louder.

In less than a minute, the first diseased's shrieks called to them from across the meadow. "Put your backs together," William said, his spear raised. "As long as we hold our formation, they won't be able to get to us."

Max on one side of him, Artan on the other, William stepped back until the five of them formed a tight ring.

The swish of long grass heralded the approach of the first diseased. It ran like many of them, stumbling at the very edge of its balance, leaning forwards with its arms windmilling. Several more appeared from different angles. They were closing in fast.

The drumbeats turned into rolls, and the hunters screamed and yelled. A celebration as wild as any inside Umbriel's walls. Still short of breath from the run, William tried to remember Greg's instruction. He gripped his spear, firm but relaxed.

The closest diseased got to within fifteen feet before a spear flew from a tree. It shot through the side of the thing's face, altering its course so it sailed past William and his friends before finally dropping into the long grass.

Another spear took down the next one.

More diseased appeared, more spears shooting from the trees.

"Hold on to your weapons," William said. "Let the hunters take them down. We might need to fight if they fail."

A hunter missed and a diseased broke through. Both of his hands on the spear's shaft, William jumped forward and drove the flint tip through the bottom of its jaw. It burst through the top of the thing's head in an eruption of blood and bone.

Returning to his friends, he leaned towards Max. "You might need to do something here. I'm not sure we'll survive otherwise."

As if answering William's call, Max sprang forward to take down the next diseased. He lunged with his spear, drove it through the eye of one of the creatures, and pulled it back out again before the thing fell. Back next to William, he said, "Trust me. If I need to, and if it will help, then I will."

"You need to."

"We're at the mercy of the hunters here. The diseased won't go away until they stop, no matter what I do."

The five of them fought as more diseased evaded the hunters, who still took down at least ninety percent of the encroaching creatures. But it only took one bite.

The drumming stopped and the flow of diseased slowed. Samson stamped his foot on the ground and threw his arms wide as he implored Slate's tree. "What the hell are you doing? This isn't what we agreed!"

Artan raised his eyebrows at William. Before William could react, the hunters jumped from the trees.

Slate smiled as wide as ever. "You can see how great this spot is for hunting. This is how we get so much meat. Anything running through here is lucky to get out of the other side alive."

"You could have shown us another way," William said. "Your little performance seemed a bit unnecessary."

"But there's nothing like a live demonstration."

While Slate talked, Hawk marched past him. Despite Olga temporarily lifting his mood, a deep frown once again dominated his features. He moved with purpose, heading straight towards Max. The punch came from nowhere, knocking Max to the ground.

William stepped forwards, Slate's spear flashing up in front of his face, the bloody tip of it just inches from his left eye. "I'd stay there if I were you."

Hawk leaned over Max before kicking him in the stomach, driving a deep "oomph" from him. "This is for shoving me over, you prick." Another hard kick. "This is payback for us having to deal with your bullshit. Who the hell do you think we are?" He made every point with a kick. "Women don't play tri-rings. Women don't hunt. And when I get back to Umbriel, I'm going to show your little bitch what women are good for."

Dropping to his knees, Hawk grabbed Max beneath his armpits and pulled him upright. Max's eyes rolled and his head flopped. Blood coated the bottom half of his face. "This is for making me clean your feet." He headbutted Max, his forehead meeting Max's nose with a *crunch!* When he let go of him, Max fell limp.

Slate grinned at William while the other hunters closed in. They outnumbered William and his friends at least five to one. William led the way in throwing down his weapons and raising his hands while Samson switched sides, joining the hunters. "Artan told me you were a snake. I should have—"

A ringing chimed through William's skull when Slate punched him. His legs weakened, but he remained on his feet long enough to take another blow. The impact slammed white light through his vision before his world turned dark.

CHAPTER 35

Willliam gasped as he choked on the frigid water. He rolled over, his left arm falling from the platform and hanging down. Artan caught him before the rest of his body followed, grabbed him by his shoulders, and spoke a gentle reassurance to him. "You're okay. Breathe."

Other than Matilda, no one could calm him as quickly. To look into the steady gaze of the boy he knew so well brought William's heart rate down and helped him find his breaths.

Artan eased William to his feet. His legs still weak, he leaned on the boy to remain upright. Now he'd regained consciousness, the world began to make sense again, a throbbing ache running through his face from where Slate had punched him. The sounds of the diseased came at them from every angle. Their rich vinegar reek hung heavy in the air. Max and Cyrus were also with them. They were standing on a broken plinth made from the same grey stone he'd seen everywhere in the ruined city. They were about ten feet from the ground. Two horses and carriages like they'd used to get through Edin were in front of them. Ranger, Magma, Samson, and Slate stood on one. Warrior, Crush, and Trent on the other.

Behind them, the cage he and Olga had rescued the others from when they went through the tunnels; in front, the hill they'd scaled. Magma's fortress lay on the other side of the hill.

With four of them on the plinth, they had room to stand up and turn around, but nothing more. Hundreds of diseased gathered around them like they had his friends in the cage. They had nowhere to hide and no escape.

The loud ringing of a bell, it jangled through William, setting his already shot nerves on edge. Thank god Artan still had a hold of him, keeping him steady while he made sense of the world. Ranger continued ringing his bell, leaning back with his laughter, his fat mouth spread wide.

William turned to his friends first, Max stumbling where William nudged him before Artan grabbed his shirt and pulled him back. A nod passed between them.

William said, "What the hell is this?" But before they answered him, he turned to Samson. "You snake! This is your doing. What have you done? Where are Matilda and Olga? Where are the other hunters?"

Still laughing, Ranger stopped ringing his bell and took a moment to compose himself. He pressed the back of his hand to his nose as if it would help contain his glee. "This is payback, Spike."

"That name died with my old life."

"This is payback for all of your bullshit during national service. For the trials and how you and your muggy little friend Hugh behaved. Where is he?"

As much as William wanted to hide his sagging frame at the mention of his friend, he couldn't fight the gravitational pull.

"Well, he's better off dead. Otherwise, I would have made him pay for leaving Edin's gates open." Ranger flicked his hand at William and the others on the plinth. "It would have been worse than this. This is all his stupid fault, after all."

"As wonderful as this little monologue is, Ranger, what the hell do you want?"

"I won't be hurried. In case you haven't noticed, we hold all the cards here." While Ranger talked, the white horse pulling his carriage shifted, making the boy and those next to him sway with its movement. "Good job the protectors built a fortress, eh?"

"While they conned Edin's residents into thinking they were worth something?" William said.

Magma wrung Jezebel's handle, his already furrowed monobrow twisting harder.

"The protectors knew there were liabilities like Hugh living in Edin." Ranger shrugged. "As much as they wanted to protect the place, there was only so much they could do. They needed to have a plan B."

The others let Ranger speak. The boy had clearly been waiting a long time to deliver what sounded like a well-rehearsed condemnation of everything William stood for. The large black horse on the other carriage stepped several feet closer, several diseased screaming louder as they were crushed beneath its steps.

Cyrus yelled, startling William as the boy leaped from the plinth. Artan reached after him too late.

The gap seemed impossibly wide, but the boy made it, belly-flopping onto the roof of Trent's carriage, his legs slamming against the wooden side with a *whack!* The large black horse grew agitated. The diseased shrieked and reached up at him, their hands beating against the carriage's wooden panelling. Before Cyrus could pull himself onto the roof, Warrior grabbed the back of his shirt and dragged him onto the carriage. He spun him over and slammed several blows into his face.

Max should have made that jump, not Cyrus. If the boy read

William's silent accusation, he ignored it.

Trent clambered into the driver's seat, his long and slim body arachnid in its movements as he crossed the gap from the carriage to the bench. He steered his carriage closer to Ranger's. Warrior and Crush dragged Cyrus up by lifting him from beneath his armpits. He hung like a rag doll, his body limp, blood dripping from his chin.

"Take him back to the fortress," Magma said. "We should make an example of him. This is what happens to deserters. Trent, you will behead him in front of everyone."

Trent's already pale skin turned several shades paler as he acquiesced to Magma's request with a nod. He clicked at the horse, much like William had with Goliath, and turned them around before taking Cyrus, Crush, and Warrior towards the hill leading to Magma's fortress.

Ranger grinned. The same smug face William had wanted to punch every single day of national service. "Well, it looks to me like you've lost, young man."

"Screw you."

"But we'll come and visit. I reckon you might last a few days up here, keeping the diseased entertained and out of our way while we continue to build our walls." The loud clanging bell pulled William's shoulders into his neck. It riled up the diseased, aggravating another strong waft of rot and vinegar.

For most of Ranger's speech, William fixed on Samson. "You're going to pay for this."

As pleased with himself as Ranger, Samson giggled. "I can't believe you fell for it. We have a deal, you see. The hunters provide our society with meat, and we provide Grandfather Jacks with women."

"You mean girls?" William said. "We saw those young girls with Rayne."

Samson shrugged. "Females. Normally, it's quite a straightforward process, but when we saw you leave Edin, we asked a little more of our friendship with Umbriel. Seeing as you and Ranger had history, it made it more personal. We wanted to have fun with you. Make you feel like you were getting somewhere, and all the while, we were waiting, ready to screw you over." The large bald man grinned.

"What happened to the Samson we met in the arena? The Samson who was a great leader of people. Where's he gone?"

"He was lost with the one hundred from the arena."

"What really happened to them?"

"I saw an opportunity and took it. Good guys and bad guys? What kind of binary bullshit is that? The only distinction in this world now is dead or alive; I choose the latter. While they were being attacked, I left."

"You abandoned them? You said you couldn't help them."

While jamming one of his thick thumbs into his chest, Samson's voice shook. "I probably couldn't have. So I chose to live, William. Judge me from the afterlife if you so wish. You might get bored waiting for me to show up though. I'm a survivor."

There seemed little point in continuing the conversation.

Ranger said, "We've been watching you for days. It's been so much fun. We watched you and Olga follow the bait we laid for you in that cage over there. We made you think you'd been so clever in rescuing your friends. Why didn't you go through the tunnels first? Actually, I don't really care. We used Samson to let you into the fortress, to make you think he was onside. We even let Cyrus join you, not that he knew anything about it. We sent you to Umbriel and they agreed to make you think you were good enough hunters to join them." He winked at Max. "Hawk wanted to keep Olga."

Slate snorted a laugh. "And we had so much fun shaving your heads."

Samson moved so quickly, the first William knew of Slate tumbling from the carriage came when he screamed as he fell. Scores of diseased smothered him, hiding him from sight.

Magma raised Jezebel and turned on Samson. "What the hell was that about?"

"They shaved my head."

"Of course they did. They needed to make it convincing."

"But—"

Magma kicked Samson with such force he lifted from the roof of the carriage before falling into the mob below. The diseased smothered the big man as easily as they'd smothered Slate.

Just Magma and his son remained. After a few seconds, William threw his arms wide. "So where are Matilda and Olga?"

Ranger stood ashen faced, peering down on the now diseased Samson and Slate. Magma stepped forward, his thick hair tousled by the wind. "They've gone to be with Grandfather Jacks."

"He's a real person?"

"Yep. And he's as mad as a box of frogs. Your little girl-friends are about to find out *all* about him. The other hunters have already returned to Umbriel so they can send them on their way. Maybe Hawk will have some fun with Olga first."

"I've had enough!" Max then said. "I'm done."

And maybe there hadn't been a better time than now. At least he'd finally chosen to do it. William stood aside while Max kneeled down on the rough stone plinth, turned around and slipped off it backwards.

Ranger laughed to watch the boy take his own life. "You're pathetic, you know that? Spike was always febrile during national service, and you were always weaker than him."

The second Max landed amongst the diseased, he charged

Ranger and Magma's carriage. Barging the diseased aside, he used the step along the bottom of the carriage to boost himself. He reached out and grabbed Ranger's right ankle.

Boom. Ranger landed on his back, the white horse twitching. Max dragged Ranger off, the boy reaching out to hold on too late, screaming as he vanished under a blanket of diseased.

A deep yell, Magma swung at Max, missing him, a wave of splinters bursting away from the gash he hacked into the carriage's roof.

Max stepped on the windowsill, pushed up, and grabbed the front of Magma's shirt. He pulled the protector off the carriage with him.

Magma landed a punch on Max before the diseased swarmed him. And a good job, because Max's eyes were glazed when he got to his feet. One more blow would have knocked him out cold.

"Get control of the carriage," William yelled.

Clarity shone through Max's glaze. He climbed the carriage again, using the embedded Jezebel as a handle to pull himself up.

Still out of breath when he reached them, Max said, "I told you I'd use my invulnerability at the right time."

"Right time?" William said. "We've just lost Cyrus."

"I couldn't have attacked them when there were two carriages. It's a good job Samson and Slate went too. Any more than two of them and I wouldn't have stood a chance."

Artan jumped across to the carriage's roof first, William hopping over a second later. From the driver's seat, Max held the reins up, but William shook his head. He couldn't form a bond with another horse like he had with Goliath.

"We need to get to Umbriel now," Max said. "Hopefully we can get to Olga and Matilda before anything happens."

Artan shook his head. "We need to get Cyrus first. Matilda's my sister, and I love her more than anything, but we can't pass Magma's fortress and leave him there. I hate to think what they'll do if we don't rescue him."

The anxiety in William's stomach had claws. They couldn't delay getting to Matilda and Olga. But he still nodded. "Artan's right. Cyrus just put himself on the line for us." He turned to Matilda's brother. "I'm sorry I didn't trust you about Samson sooner. You had his number from the start."

"We'll make it right. We'll save him and we'll get Tilly and Olga back."

"Can you lead us over that hill, Max?" William said. "We need to think of a way to get in and out of the fortress as quickly as possible."

Max lay on his front on the roof of the carriage, William and Artan on either side of him as he led them towards the hill. The diseased were furious beneath them, but they were already losing interest now they couldn't see them. Hopefully they'd leave the mob behind.

They passed Ranger on his right side. Now one of the diseased masses, the boy had several deep and glistening cuts on his face from where he'd been bitten. "Magma deserved everything he got," William said, "but I can't help feeling sorry for Ranger, even after everything. He was a sad little boy with no mum and a sociopath for a dad. They might have been tracking us for most of the time, but Olga and I saw how Magma spoke to him. The bullying seemed real. Ranger could never meet his dad's expectations. He could have been someone very different had he been dealt better cards." Diseased's screams, the familiar sway of the carriage, the midday sun beating down on them as the three fell into silence.

Max halted the carriage and slipped from the roof. The creatures had no interest in him, Ranger damn near oblivious as he slipped the boy's sword and sheath from his back. He passed it up to William before taking his place in the middle again.

William hugged the weapon. "As much as I got used to having a spear, it feels good to have a sword again. Artan, you take Jezebel. I think we'll be glad of these weapons soon."

CHAPTER 36

Now they were close to the back wall of Magma's fortress, William lifted his head. There were only a few diseased nearby, and none of them noticed him. "Well, at least it's got us here without a fan club. Now we need to get through this as quickly as possible. Get in, get out, and get Olga and Matilda away from Umbriel."

Both Max and Artan nodded.

They were about eight feet from the ground on the roof of the carriage. Not much lower than the spiked perimeter of Magma's fortress. "There are huts over this back wall," William said. "We jump it and we'll land on the roofs."

Artan and Max stared at him.

"I'll go first."

Artan and Max nodded.

In one fluid movement, William hopped up into a crouch, gripped one of the spiked points along the top of the wall, and vaulted over. Despite his prior knowledge, his stomach still leaped into his throat as he fell down the other side. A split second of doubt. What if the huts were farther along?

His fall was halted by the roofs of the huts he knew to be

there. The shock of his landing ran up through his legs, and William rolled aside as Artan and then Max followed him over. Both of them had jumped blind, trusting his judgement.

When Max tried to stand up, William pulled him back down again. All three of them lay along the roof, William pointing up its slant. "The angle of these roofs means those on guard can't see us as long as we stay down."

Led by William, all three of them crawled on their stomachs up the roof's slant and peered over the edge at the community. A crowd of maybe sixty had gathered by the main gates. A good chunk of the population. William said, "They must be waiting for Magma and Ranger's carriage to return."

"How long before they realise they're not going to?" Max said.

"Hopefully long enough for us to get Cyrus the hell out of here."

A tap on his shoulder, William followed where Artan pointed. Over by the fire, near the beheading block, stood Cyrus, his hands bound behind his back. Trent hovered close by, an executioner's axe in his grip. The sight of the beanpole boy turned the acid in William's stomach. Sure, he'd been the one to punch Trent when he'd wanted to get out of Edin, and he had to take responsibility for his part in their dispute, but Trent had taken it to a whole new level. "That's good."

Max lifted his head to see Cyrus before pulling back down again. "Doesn't look very good."

"No, you're right," William said. "It looks like they're getting Cyrus ready to behead him. Olga and I had to watch them do it when we were in here looking for you three. They beheaded two boys and took a girl away. She must have been a gift for Grandfather Jacks. But what's good about it is Cyrus is close to the back gate. Artan and I will go and free him while you go through it and clear a path on the other side. You can make sure we have a clear run. Also, as much as I hate this community, I'd rather not fight my way through it. Most of these people might have made a choice I wouldn't have made, but they're just trying to survive. The fact that Cyrus is away from the pack is a huge advantage."

"You want me to get the horse?" Max said.

"I think we should go on foot. It might keep us away from the diseased on the carriage, but if we use it there are only certain paths we can take. I think it'll slow us down too much. Make us too easy to catch."

Ranger's sword sheathed on his back, William crawled along the roofs towards the fire, Artan taking up the rear while maintaining a grip on Jezebel.

When they reached the end, William pointed at the back gate. "Max, you get that open and we'll get Cyrus. You both ready?"

Max gave William a thumbs up. Artan stared steel at him.

It didn't matter how he focused on his breaths, William couldn't force calm. Better to use the adrenaline than try to suppress it, he slipped from the roof, landed on the ground, and sprinted towards the fire. Trent turned in time to take a hard shove in the chest, the boy's long arms windmilling as he dropped his axe and fell to the ground.

While Artan freed Cyrus, William levelled Ranger's sword on Trent's throat. "Scream and I'll end you."

"Let's go," Artan said, dragging Cyrus towards Max at the back gate.

A tight grip on his sword's handle, the tip of it shook, hovering just inches from ending Trent. He could silence him before he gave them away. But he couldn't. The past few days had been a fight to survive. What point would there be in living if he lost his humanity? Instead, he kicked Trent in the head, knocking the boy out cold before dragging his long form away from the fire and out of sight behind the small woodshed.

Cyrus, Max, and Artan all stood at the back gate. When William got closer, he said, "What are you doing?"

"They've nailed it shut," Max said, tugging the handle as if to prove his point.

William tugged on the gate's handle too. The silver glint of different shaped bent nails ran all the way down one side. It would take them too long to pull them out.

"Let's get back on the roof of the huts. We can—"

A group of about eight men and women appeared. Led by Warrior, they cut off their route.

William's heart sank. "Shit."

CHAPTER 37

"What do we do, William?" Max said. "I don't have a weapon to fight them."

And neither did Cyrus.

"Follow me." William took off towards the fire, Warrior's group tracking their progress.

"We can't fight them, William."

A shovel rested near the fire. It had been fashioned from an old sheet of metal, the head of it covered in ash. William dug it into the fire's embers and threw the red-hot coals at the pack closing in on them.

Several of them screamed, and then screamed again when he launched another shovelful. But that wouldn't hold them back indefinitely. He handed the shovel to Cyrus. "Use this to keep them busy."

While Cyrus sent another shower of coals at Warrior's group, Artan stood ready with Jezebel. William grabbed Max. "We need to go out the front, and you need to lead the way."

Those waiting for Ranger and Magma's return were still gathered by the gates. Far enough away to be aware of the commotion, but hopefully they hadn't yet worked out what caused it.

William shoved Max. "Go!"

Cyrus threw more fire at Warrior. When the protector covered his face, Artan lunged at him, burying Jezebel's curved blade into the top of his head. His skull cracked like a diseased's and the man went down, taking the battle-axe with him. Artan grabbed Warrior's war hammer and slammed its thick head into two more of the group.

"Catch!" William said, throwing his sword at Cyrus' feet before running to be at Artan's side, liberating Jezebel from Warrior's skull.

The rest of Warrior's group ran towards the masses at the gate. Max had gotten close to them too. If William left it too much longer, his friend would be screwed. "Diseased!" he shrieked, and several people screamed.

William led Artan and Cyrus towards the front gates. He waved his arms in the air. "There are diseased in here. Get out! Get out now!"

The group opened the gates for them, Cyrus and Artan stoking the panic with him. "Diseased! Diseased!"

They joined the mass exodus, a shrill cry of Magma's community running into the creatures outside the gates.

The second he ran outside, someone grabbed William's arm. He raised Jezebel, halting just before he swung it at Max.

Max dragged William along the wall, away from the gates and away from the rapidly turning crowd.

They reached the end of the front wall and darted around the corner, Artan ending a diseased with a swing of his war hammer. Clear of the chaos and their immediate vicinity free of diseased, they all fought for breath and took a moment.

"You all okay?" William said.

Each one nodded in turn.

"Good. Now that was hard, but we don't have time to hang around. We need to get to Matilda and Olga before they're taken to Grandfather Jacks."

They all needed longer to recover, but William led them away, and they all followed. They had to use every ounce of strength to get to the girls before it was too late.

CHAPTER 38

W ith the ruined city well behind them and William's lungs damn near ready to burst, he led the group in slowing down to a walk. His hands on his hips, the rain stinging as it slammed down against his head and face, he spoke in gasps as he tried to recover. "I'm sorry, but I'm going to have a heart attack if I keep running."

Artan stopped a few steps ahead of William and turned back, ready to argue. But when he looked from Cyrus to Max, both of them as exhausted as William, he let it go. The months in a cell had left him so skinny he'd snap if he fell, but the boy could still outrun them all.

The rain turned William's trousers heavy with damp, but at least it washed away the war paint that marked them as a part of Umbriel's community. Artan stepped aside so William could lead them again, walking through the long grass up a slight incline. Again, he faced the sky and opened his mouth, his thirst quenched by the slightly muddy taste.

After a few minutes of walking, William, Max, and Cyrus managed to get their breathing on a par with Artan's.

"Some of those people didn't deserve that," Cyrus said,

droplets of rainwater hanging from his eyelashes. "There were a lot of decent folk in Magma's community."

William's jaw ached from clamping it against the chill. "But how could we make the distinction in the chaos? We had to get out of there, and half the people wanted us dead."

"I dunno, but a lot of them were good people is all I'm saying. I might have only spent a day or two with them, but most of them hated how Magma ran the place."

"Yet they made the choice to stay," Max said.

"They were safe. That means a lot in this world. Not all of them were like Trent, you know?"

Before Max sniped back, William said, "Let's hope the good ones survived. I'm sad for them, I really am, but we need to focus on what's ahead." He cleared his throat to maintain a strong voice. "We can't dwell on all that's passed. Not yet anyway."

The meadow stretched out in front of them as they crested the hill, Umbriel standing strong against the windy raining onslaught.

"What the hell?" Artan said, squinting against the weather. "Who's that?"

"Oh, shit," William said. He waited until they were closer to Umbriel's castled front. The man had been thrown over the side, his corpse hanging by a rope tied around his neck. "It's Greg."

"I'm sorry, man." Artan put his long and skinny arm around William. "I know you and he were friends."

William nodded and looked away. After a few seconds, he said, "We need to find where Olga and Matilda are and put this place behind us."

"What's the plan?" Max said. "I can't see them lifting the gate for us."

The cries of several diseased cut through their discussion.

No matter how long William had spent around the things, the noise always snapped him rigid.

Cyrus raised Ranger's sword. William gripped Jezebel. Artan held his war hammer ready to swing.

"What about you?" Cyrus said.

Max shrugged. "I'm invulnerable to their bites. That's how we took down Ranger and Magma and got you out of their fortress."

Even over the rain and howling wind, the diseased tore through the grass with a *whoosh*. Their mouths were spread wide, ready to deliver toxic bites. Flailing arms. Crimson stares.

"Why didn't you tell me sooner?"

"Now's not the time, Cyrus," William said as he stepped forward and hacked down the first of the pack, Artan attacking by his side.

One slipped past William, and Cyrus missed it. Max swiped its legs away so it fell face first into the grass.

As Cyrus stabbed the thing through the back of the head, he said, "It didn't even want to bite you."

"Focus, Cyrus!" William took down another diseased. Artan slammed the heavy end of his hammer into the face of two of them, one after the other, with two swinging uppercuts.

All of them down, Cyrus remained focused on Max. "So why did I jump onto Trent's carriage if you could have gotten off the plinth at any point?"

"I didn't ask you to do it."

"Look," Artan said, stepping between the two of them, "if you hadn't, Max wouldn't have been able to take down Magma and Ranger. Samson kicked Slate from the roof because he shaved his head, and Magma kicked Samson off for killing Slate. Max could surprise two of them, but he couldn't have done anything about seven. You helped because you took a large part of the threat away."

"We need to go around the back," William said.

It killed the conversation.

"I know it's getting late," William continued, the dark clouds combining with the fading light of late afternoon, "but Rita and Mary could still be working in the field."

"Uh …" Max said. "There's a massive fence in the way."

"We don't need to get in. We just need to talk to them. We need to know if Olga and Matilda are still in there. Come on, let's go."

THE ALREADY STINGING RAIN FELL EVEN HARDER, EVERY DROP striking William's head like a hammer against a nail. They'd given the place a wide enough berth to remain hidden from sight, and they now approached it at a crouch.

The large drum a part of the back wall, spear tips visible over the spiked perimeter from where a new batch stood in the bucket for the trials. If there were any watchmen on the scaffolding, they hid themselves well.

William's eyes stung as his sweat mixed with the rainwater cascading down his face. When he reached the back wall, he leaned against it. The tall and sharpened tree trunks that made up Umbriel's perimeter provided ample defence against the diseased, but because of their natural shape, there were gaps between each one. William peered through one of the gaps. "There they are!"

But just before he could call out, a single drumbeat slammed above them. All four of them pressed their backs against the wooden fence and looked up. William leaned out to see who made the noise. "I can only see one of them."

"It's not them we should be worried about," Max said.

A diseased had already reacted to the first beat. It appeared as if from nowhere and charged. It headed straight for them. William raised Jezebel while Artan and Cyrus readied their weapons.

A spear slammed through its face, knocking it to the ground and killing it dead.

The aspiring hunter beat the drum again.

"Why doesn't he just piss off?" Artan said.

"Max," William said, "I need you to be our first line of defence here, okay?" But he didn't wait for Max's reply, instead he pressed his face to the gap in the fence and hissed through it. "Mary! Rita!"

Several more drumbeats drowned him out, so he waited for a lull and tried louder than before. "Mary! Rita!"

Both women stopped and turned to the fence.

"It's William. I'm out here with Max, Artan—"

The drumming started up again. When it finally stopped, the shriek of a diseased ran gooseflesh down William's spine.

"Justin!" Mary called up at the scaffolding. "I've got a headache. Can you give it a rest for today?"

A voice breaking from where Justin was clearly transitioning from an adolescent to a young man. "But I need to practice."

Balled fists on her ample hips, Mary glared at him. "Don't make me come up there and kick your arse."

"Come on, Mary, I really want to make the next trials."

While pinching the top of her nose, feigning a headache, Mary spoke at the ground. "Just for today. *Please?*"

The diseased was about thirty feet away from them.

"Just this one more?"

"Say yes, Mary," William whispered.

"No! Not today."

"Shit!" She clearly hadn't heard him.

Twenty-five feet away. Justin remained on the wall, the tip of his spear visible from below. He then pulled it away.

"Come on, Justin," Rita said. "Hurry it up."

"All right, I'm doing it."

"Don't get wide with me, young man!"

Fifteen feet away, its blood red glaze fixed on William and his friends.

Max twisted his feet as if to sure up his stance while William leaned away from the wall. He held a halting hand at Max while he watched Justin.

Ten feet.

The boy vanished from sight and William said, "Now!"

Max rugby tackled the diseased, slamming his shoulder into its gut. The thing belched a rancid waft of vinegar rot.

The diseased twisted and writhed while Max pinned it down. Cyrus stabbed it through the face.

No more diseased around, William returned to the gap in the fence and watched Mary and Rita wave Justin away.

After they'd watched the boy out of sight, the two women moved close to the fence. Rita said, "Matilda and Olga have already gone."

"What? When?"

"This morning. Shortly after you were taken out hunting. Carl and Peter, two of the retired hunters, took them." Rita paused as if to compose herself. Her eyes filled with tears. "They've been taken to Grandfather Jacks."

"Shit. Why didn't you tell us more about him?" William said. "You could have warned us."

Mary's eyes also glazed. "You saw what happened to Greg, right? Someone was listening to your conversations and they found out he told you to get away from the community. Someone's *always* listening here. This is our home, William. We've been through the worst of it with Grandfather Jacks. As long as we work here, we're safe. We can't jeopardise that. We wouldn't survive out there. We're really sorry."

"Sorry won't get my sister back."

William eased Artan away with a gentle shove. "What are they going to do to Matilda and Olga?"

"Nothing yet," Rita said.

"Why?"

"It's not a full moon. He chooses a new bride on every full moon."

"A bride? What the hell?"

"Well, bride suggests some sort of consent. Sometimes, he chooses multiple brides."

Cyrus pressed his face to another gap. "But some of those girls taken from Magma's fortress were just kids."

Rita turned his way. "The younger, the better. And it's even worse for the boys he chooses. Hawk used to be one of Grandfather Jacks' *angels*."

Although he'd been watching their backs, Max leaned close to the gap. "Is that where his scars came from?"

Her eyes bloodshot, Rita swiped her damp blonde hair away from her face. "Yeah. He's one of the few Grandfather Jacks didn't kill afterwards. When I look into that boy's eyes, sometimes I wonder if he would have been better off dead."

"When's the next full moon?" William said.

"Three days' time."

William pulled out his map and hunched over it, shielding it from the rain.

"Where did you get that?" Mary said.

"We found it on someone a while back. Can you show us where they've gone?"

"That one there," Mary said. "Diagonally down to the left from here." The community had been marked on the map as a square about half the size of Umbriel. It had a box by it that—while still green—had a slightly redder tinge.

"It looks like it's miles away. Much farther than Umbriel is from Edin," Artan said.

"It'll take you a day or two to walk it."

William swiped the water from his head. Because of his lack of hair, it ran into his eyes again seconds later. "We need to get moving. We need to get there before the next full moon."

As if praying, Rita pressed her hands together. "We're sorry we didn't tell you about this sooner. We wish you all the luck in the world."

William spoke through his tightly clamped jaw. "We don't need luck. We're going to find Grandfather Jacks, and we're going to cut his fucking head off."

END OF BOOK FIVE.

Thank you for reading *After Edin - Book five of Beyond These Walls.*

**Book six - *Three Days* - Is available to order now.
Go to www.michaelrobertson.co.uk**

Support the Author

Dear reader, as an independent author I don't have the resources of a huge publisher. If you like my work and would like to see more from me in the future, there are two things you can do to help: leaving a review, and a word-of-mouth referral.

Releasing a book takes many hours and hundreds of dollars. I love to write, and would love to continue to do so. All I ask is that you leave an Amazon review. It shows other readers that you've enjoyed the book and will encourage them to give it a try too. The review can be just one sentence, or as long as you like.

If you've enjoyed Beyond These Walls you may also enjoy my other post-apocalyptic series. The Alpha Plague: Books 1-8 (the complete series) are available now.

The Alpha Plague - Available Now at www. michaelrobertson.co.uk

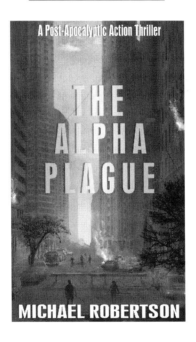

Or save money by picking up the entire series box set.

Chapter One

The hard rain assaulted Olga, coming down on her as if nails were being fired from the clouds. It forced her to walk with a stoop, but at least she slowly sated her thirst, her tongue poked out to catch the muddy-tasting water. Her thin layer of clothes clung to her like a second skin, and she shivered from the biting cold, her muscles tense, cramps streaking up the side of her face from how hard she clamped her jaw. A hard kick to her lower back sent her stumbling several steps forwards. She pulled against her tight bonds, the rope wrapped around her wrists cutting into her skin. Her hands bound behind her back, she clenched them into fists and spoke through gritted teeth. "I'm walking! What more do you want from me?"

About six feet two inches tall, Carl had white hair and a fat face. Waxy skin with ruddy cheeks, his green eyes were stone cold in stark contrast to his wonky and yellow-toothed grin. He wore jeans and a shirt with a high collar that poked from the top of his sodden coat. The top few buttons of his shirt were undone, revealing scars similar to the ones Hawk had around his neck.

Matilda—her hands bound like Olga's—shoulder barged her friend to encourage her forwards. "He's just trying to get a reaction from you."

Olga took Matilda's guidance and moved on, but she wouldn't be silenced. "Maybe I *should* react. Show these pricks we can't be pushed around."

"I'm not sure that would send the correct message in our current state." Matilda shrugged as if to highlight her restricted mobility.

Peter—the other retired hunter tasked with taking them to Grandfather Jacks—walked beside Carl. Much shorter than the large angry man, he stood at around five feet and six inches and had skin as dark as William's. Different to Carl in almost every way, the most striking feature to mark him out resided in his compassionate face, his brown feline eyes glowing with a serenity absent from Carl's chaotic stare. This task clearly gave him little pleasure, and he spoke with a soft voice. "You might want to listen to your friend."

Like Olga should trust the good cop, bad cop routine. They were both horrible bastards. Forget that and she might as well walk herself to Grandfather Jacks. Aches ran across her gums when she bit down harder. A flick of her head to keep her hair from her face, Olga said, "Screw Max."

"Huh?" Matilda said.

"I can't stop thinking about what he's done. Screw him." Olga's pulse quickened and her breaths grew shallow. "He made me look like a fool in front of everyone."

"But—"

"Don't you dare excuse him."

"I wasn't going to, but how's thinking that way helping us right now? You should try to stay calm."

"How will being calm help?" Before Matilda could reply, Olga raised her voice. "The last thing I need is to be calm. I'm going to be ready for war. What kind of ridiculous name is Grandfather Jacks anyway?"

Although Olga winced in anticipation of another kick from Carl, Peter's calm words met her question. "He's the High Father. The prophet. The only one amongst us who can commune with heaven."

"That sounds like bullshit to me. Besides, if there is a god, or High Father, or whatever you decide to call her, I'd say she left us a long time ago."

"*He*," Peter said.

"And you know that for a fact, do you?"

"In my heart." Peter drew a deep and calming breath as if feeling the presence of his god inside him. "Anyway, all will be revealed in time."

"You'll introduce me to the big man, will you?"

"We will all meet our maker in the end."

Already sodden, the long grass dragged on Olga's steps, seeds coating her soaked trousers. "That's a convenient way of avoiding the issue. You don't know the answers to any of life's big questions. None of us do. You might have faith in your convictions, and I might even be able to respect that should you choose to present them in that way, but to offer them as facts? You—" Olga's words were cut short by another shove. It sent her several paces forwards before she slammed down, her knees sinking into the muddy ground.

Another hard blow into the centre of her back, Olga fell face first into the grass. Fire ripped through her shoulder blades when Carl pulled her bound wrists, forcing her nose into the ground. Mud on her lips and in her mouth, she fought the urge to scream. Don't give them the satisfaction.

Peter positioned himself between Carl and Olga, forcing the

sadistic guard to let go. He then lifted her to her feet, a hand beneath each armpit. "Now get up and shut up."

When Olga stood upright, Carl shoved Peter aside and kicked her a second time. She ran at the edge of her balance, tugging against her bonds until she finally fell again, face first onto the ground.

Squelching footsteps closed in on Olga. She rolled onto her back and lifted her knees. But Matilda prevented Carl from reaching her, shoulder barging him aside, so his kick hit thin air instead of the intended target of Olga's head.

For a second time Peter got between Carl and the girls and held his hands up as if to calm his fellow guard. "Think about what Grandfather Jacks will say if you beat these two black and blue."

His green eyes wide, his nostrils flared, Carl's barrel chest rose and fell with his heavy pants. He loomed over the smaller man. If he so desired, he'd overpower him in an instant. The rain had turned his thin white hair so damp it revealed his pink scalp beneath. "You think I give a shit about what he thinks?"

Adrenaline surged through Olga as she got to her feet and shivered, awaiting Carl's next outburst.

A gentler shove, Peter encouraged Olga forwards. "Move before this situation gets away from all of us."

A nauseating clamp to her stomach as they set off again, Olga spoke so only Matilda heard. "I promise you, before these clowns can deliver us to Grandfather Jacks, I'm going to cut both their throats."

"And if the moment comes, I'll be right beside you." Her brown eyes calm, Matilda said, "But for now, we have to accept they're the ones in control. Besides, we don't know what's happening with the boys."

"Are you saying we should wait to be rescued? Firstly, how the hell will they know where we are? It would be quite a lucky guess for them to find us. Secondly, I'm no damsel in distress. I plan on getting *myself* out of this."

"I'm saying we should pick our moment, and it isn't now."

"Less talking, more walking," Carl said. "You two don't know how lucky you are, let me tell you."

"Don't," Matilda said, catching Olga's reply before it left her mouth.

Carl continued. "I've heard what some of the hunters do with their hostages before delivering them to Grandfather Jacks."

"But we're not those types of guards." Although Peter aimed his words at the girls, he clearly meant them for Carl. The deep-voiced sadist grumbled an indecipherable response to his friend. Hopefully an acceptance. Olga hated the fact, but Matilda was right. The odds were not in their favour.

Olga breathed through her nose and shook her head. "I will wait for the right moment, but I swear, they will die at my hand."

"What's that, little one?" Carl said.

Matilda stepped closer to Olga. "And I'll be at your side when the moment's right."

The meadow stretched out ahead of them, the wind controlling the long grass. Olga's eyes stung with tiredness, grief, and the glow of the rising sun as it found gaps in the grey clouds.

Olga might have let it go, but Carl clearly hadn't. Even though she refused to look at the vile man, she heard the grin in his voice. "Come on, little one. Surely you have more fight in you? Tell me all your complaints so I can forward them to the 'I don't give a shit' department."

A surge of adrenaline turned Olga's pulse into a bass drum. She spun and charged Carl. The man might have been twice her size and have full use of his fists, but he didn't have her spirit. He smiled and dropped into a crouch, his hands balled.

The squelch of Matilda's steps joined Olga's as she joined the attack.

Spirit or not, Carl moved fast. The air left Olga's lungs. The first she knew of the blow was when it hit her stomach. Her feet lifted from the ground as she wrapped around his clenched fist. She turned weightless and flew backwards, landing bottom first with a squelch, her diaphragm locked in violent spasms.

Despite gasping for breath, Olga tried to sit up as Carl landed a right cross on Matilda's chin with a *crack!* Her friend's legs turned bandy and she crumpled.

Close to vomiting, Olga rolled forwards while Carl punched the already unconscious Matilda again. "Stop!" Olga gasped, unable to get her words out because of her need to breathe. "Stop!"

Carl kicked Matilda in the stomach, flipping her onto her back.

"Leave—" Olga got up onto one knee "—her."

Peter grabbed Carl across his chest and pulled him back.

Olga stood up, still fighting for breath. "Leave her alone, you prick." She charged Carl yet again. This time she read his attack and stepped aside, evading his blow. As the man pulled back, she jumped like a salmon, a white flash bursting through her vision when she headbutted him.

Fury glowed in Carl's glare, but before he could get to Olga, Peter stepped between them again and pushed the guard back. "Grandfather Jacks will hang us out to dry."

"I don't care!"

"I do, so stop it!"

Although Carl finally stepped back and some of the tension left his frame, he remained fixed on Olga, his shoulders rising and falling with his ragged breaths.

A stinging throb where her forehead had met Carl's nose, Olga stumbled back several steps from Peter's hard shove. She ground her teeth and remained fixed on Carl, his top lip coated with blood. Let him come at her again. See what happened.

Too fast for Peter to react, Carl sidestepped his partner and kicked Matilda in the chin. Her head snapped back. As Peter went to Matilda, Carl charged Olga. "You won't get me twice, you little shit."

A flash from where Carl punched her. Her sinuses on fire. Olga's legs gave out and her world turned dark.

Thank you for reading chapter one of Three Days - Book six of Beyond These Walls. You can get the whole book at www.michaelrobertson.co.uk

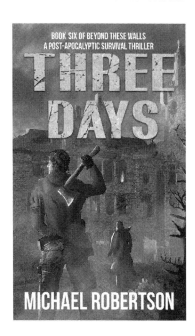

ABOUT THE AUTHOR

Like most children born in the seventies, Michael grew up with Star Wars in his life. An obsessive watcher of the films, and an avid reader from an early age, he found himself taken over with stories whenever he let his mind wander.

Those stories had to come out.

He hopes you enjoy reading his books as much as he does writing them.

Michael loves to travel when he can. He has a young family, who are his world, and when he's not reading, he enjoys walking so he can dream up more stories.

Contact
www.michaelrobertson.co.uk
subscribers@michaelrobertson.co.uk

.

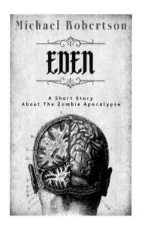

Michael Robertson

EDEN

A Short Story
About The Zombie Apocalypse

RAT RUN

A POST-APOCALYPTIC TALE

Michael Robertson

ALSO BY MICHAEL ROBERTSON

The Shadow Order

The First Mission - Book Two of The Shadow Order

The Crimson War - Book Three of The Shadow Order

Eradication - Book Four of The Shadow Order

Fugitive - Book Five of The Shadow Order

Enigma - Book Six of The Shadow Order

Prophecy - Book Seven of The Shadow Order

The Faradis - Book Eight of The Shadow Order

The Complete Shadow Order Box Set - Books 1 - 8

The Blind Spot - A Science Fiction Thriller - Neon Horizon
Book One.

Prime City - A Science Fiction Thriller - Neon Horizon Book Two.

Bounty Hunter - A Science Fiction Thriller - Neon Horizon Book
Three.

The Alpha Plague: A Post-Apocalyptic Action Thriller

The Alpha Plague 2

The Alpha Plague 3

The Alpha Plague 4

The Alpha Plague 5

The Alpha Plague 6

The Alpha Plague 7

The Alpha Plague 8

The Complete Alpha Plague Box Set - Books 1 - 8

Protectors - Book one of Beyond These Walls

National Service - Book two of Beyond These Walls

Retribution - Book three of Beyond These Walls

Collapse - Book four of Beyond These Walls

After Edin - Book five of Beyond These Walls

Three Days - Book six of Beyond These Walls

The Asylum - Book seven of Beyond These Walls

Between Fury and Fear - Book Eight of Beyond These Walls

Beyond These Walls - Books 1 - 6 Box Set

The Girl in the Woods - A Ghost's Story - Off-Kilter Tales Book One

Rat Run - A Post-Apocalyptic Tale - Off-Kilter Tales Book Two

Masked - A Psychological Horror

Crash - A Dark Post-Apocalyptic Tale

Crash II: Highrise Hell